W9-AHM-382

THE
LITTLE
BALLOONIST

THE
LITTLE
BALLOONIST

A NOVEL

LINDA DONN

DUTTON

DUTTON
Published by the Penguin Group (USA) Inc.
375 Hudson Street, New York, New York 10014, U.S.A.
Penguin Group (Canada), 90 Eglinton Avenue East, Suite 700, Toronto, Ontario, Canada M4P
2Y3 (a division of Pearson Penguin Canada Inc.); Penguin Books Ltd, 80 Strand, London
WC2R 0RL, England; Penguin Ireland, 25 St Stephen's Green, Dublin 2, Ireland (a division of
Penguin Books Ltd); Penguin Group (Australia), 250 Camberwell Road, Camberwell, Victoria
3124, Australia (a division of Pearson Australia Group Pty Ltd); Penguin Books India (Pvt) Ltd,
11 Community Centre, Panchsheel Park, New Delhi – 110 017, India; Penguin Group (NZ), cnr
Airborne and Rosedale Roads, Albany, Auckland 1310, New Zealand (a division of Pearson
New Zealand Ltd); Penguin Books (South Africa) (Pty) Ltd, 24 Sturdee Avenue, Rosebank,
Johannesburg 2196, South Africa

Penguin Books Ltd, Registered Offices: 80 Strand, London WC2R 0RL, England

Published by Dutton, a member of Penguin Group (USA) Inc.

First printing, January 2006
1 3 5 7 9 10 8 6 4 2

Page 203 constitutes on extension of the copyright page.

REGISTERED TRADEMARK—MARCA REGISTRADA

LIBRARY OF CONGRESS CATALOGING-IN-PUBLICATION DATA
Donn, Linda.
The little balloonist : a novel / Linda Donn.
p. cm.
ISBN 0-525-94928-3 (alk. paper)
1. Blanchard, Marie-Madeleine-Sophie Armand, 1778–1819—Fiction. 2. France—
History—Consulate and First Empire, 1799–1815—Fiction. 3. Napoleon I, Emperor
of the French, 1769–1821—Fiction. 4. Balloon ascensions—Fiction. 5. Women bal-
loonists—Fiction. I. Title.
PS3604.O558L58 2006
813'.6—dc22   2005023724

Printed in the United States of America
Designed by Nancy Resnick

This book is dedicated to the memory of my mother,

who is everywhere in these pages.

Janet Wirt Brown

1907–1972

CONTENTS

THE
LITTLE
BALLOONIST

PROLOGUE

ST. HELENA COULDN'T STAND UP TO the wind that tore across the South Atlantic, and few trees dotted the island's high plateau. Not for the first time Napoleon marveled that such a hot and humid place could be so bleak. He was lounging on his favorite black bench. Years before he had chopped off a slat in the back to give himself elbow room, and the hard seat didn't bother him, for he had run to fat.

"As you see, doctor, beautiful arms, rounded breasts, soft white skin," he had told Dr. Antommarchi that morning. "More than one beautiful lady would glory in a chest like that!"

Napoleon laughed, remembering the look on the young doctor's face. He unbuttoned his shirt and prepared to nap.

An hour later the exiled emperor woke at the sound of a newspaper being flipped along the slats of his bench. Napoleon was fond of little games and he kept his eyes closed as he held out his hands. Maybe today he would be lucky.

French papers came rarely to British-owned St. Helena, but maybe today he would get the news from Paris and word of the woman he loved.

The former emperor had spent his last days on French soil near the village where Sophie Armant had grown up. When his ship to exile had set sail, Napoleon had searched for the black stones of La Salière. His friend Marc-Emmanuel Duroc had told him Sophie had learned to read sitting with her mother on the beach in a hollowed-out stone, chanting into the wind the words that she got wrong. Napoleon had watched through his field glasses until the bouldered shore-line disappeared into the horizon along with the rest of the world he had lost.

The newspaper was in Napoleon's hands and his eyes were still closed, but his shoulders sagged against the hope of news. Even if there were an article about her, it would be filled with the details of Sophie's public life. It would say nothing of the girl she had been before they met and nothing of the woman she had become without him.

The things he wanted to know, and never would.

Napoleon sighed and opened his eyes, then stared at the headlines of *Le Journal de Paris*.

PART ONE

MAY 1794–AUGUST 1808

1

A LETTER ARRIVES

SHARP SALT AIR FILLED HER LUNGS and slicked across her face as sixteen-year-old Sophie Armant walked to the sea to gather mussels. She scarcely noticed the fog that smudged the line between water and sky, for she was used to a world without reference points. Her village floated on salt flats that joined the sea on a level plane and nothing grew taller than her knee.

Sophie took off her white bonnet. Made of lace and stiff with starch, it could fly in the slightest breeze. It had done so before. She tied the ribbons to her basket, pulled off her wooden shoes, and began to pick mussels from the rocks. Bare-legged, in her long black dress, she looked like a young blackbird as she darted here and there at the edge of the sea.

Soldiers and peasants were fighting in the north that spring, but little disturbed this curve of French coast tucked in a small bay. The shadows of clouds moved across an empty landscape, yet Sophie had a sense of events unfolding beyond the quiet stretch of sand; her mother had seen to that.

Though she couldn't know that one day she would figure in them.

The water was cold and the sea foamed around her. Sophie stopped to loop up her skirt and tuck the hem in the waistband of her apron, then worked quickly again, pausing only to wave to the postman on his ride from La Rochelle and glance over at the Giroux's cottage.

As usual there was no sign of her friend André.

When she had filled her basket, Sophie picked up a white shell and a black one. Years ago, she and André had played a wishing game, and now she pushed the white shell firmly into the wet sand. It meant yes. The black shell meant no, and Sophie was tempted to press it in only lightly. She debated with herself, but finally she pushed that shell in just as hard.

Usually the waves took one shell away, leaving behind the answer to her question.

Always before, Sophie had asked the shells if someday André would marry her, and she nearly asked it again, but stopped to think. Though they were the same age, he had always seemed much older, and months before, she had decided that he had lost interest in her because she was too childish. But to make sure, she asked the shells a different question. Then she watched carefully. Like most peasants, Sophie lived with magic; she would never cross a knife with a spoon or put three lighted candles on a table. And so, while she called it a game, her eyes were riveted on the shells.

Yet a few minutes later, when she picked up her basket of mussels, Sophie was no closer to knowing if André loved her, because the waves had carried away both shells at once.

After a last look at the sea, Sophie set off across the marsh. When she walked into her family's kitchen, she saw a letter lying on the table. With its thick black ink scrolling into waves, she assumed it was from a man. In her village, only boys were taught to write. They sat at a table in the front of the schoolroom and practiced their letters while the girls watched in the back.

Sophie could write because her mother had taught her.

In La Salière letters were prized, for few arrived. Often they were propped on a shelf for everyone to see, but Isabelle Armant thrust this one in the waistband of her skirt. She had been certain Jean-Pierre Blanchard had forgotten his pledge to marry her daughter. Arranged marriages were as common in the cottages of La Salière as they were in the châteaus of La Rochelle, but it had been years since she and her husband had heard from Jean-Pierre. And so it had not troubled Isabelle that Sophie's nearly first word had been André's name, and that since childhood her daughter's heart had flown across the marsh to him.

As a little girl, when Sophie dropped a spoon, André had caught it as it fell.

Isabelle could not imagine one without the other.

But now the letter had come.

Sophie mustn't marry Jean-Pierre, Isabelle thought. She would speak to her husband.

Small mysteries broke through the surface of Sophie's day.

At noon as always her father spread mussels on a weathered board and piled twigs on top. Usually she and her mother stood nearby, for the fire burned quickly and they knew when it died the mussels would be ready to eat. But today, as her father filled their plates, the letter was sticking out of his pocket and her mother was walking on the beach.

Most evenings when her parents went to bed Sophie heard only her father's dry coughing behind their closed door. Tonight they exclaimed softly to each other, and at first their words hung in the air, infused with a kind of wonder she hadn't heard before. But then her mother's voice grew sharp, until an unusual, harsh response from her father ended the conversation.

To Sophie the sound was like fabric tearing, like something that might be mended but would never be the same.

The next morning when Georges Armant announced her coming marriage, Sophie bowed her head over her bowl of coffee and said nothing. This was not a time when girls chose their husbands, and in La Salière, no one was as rich as her suitor Jean-Pierre Blanchard. Her father was too frail to work, and she and her mother barreled up the salt, but even so, with the new taxes she knew there was no money to be made.

Sophie heard the sadness in her mother's voice as she took up the story of her engagement. "One morning sixteen years ago," she said, "two months before you were born, a young man came down the path pushing a contraption made of two bicycles. He said his name was Jean-Pierre Blanchard and started telling us about his invention, when suddenly he had some sort of attack and collapsed. We made up a bed and brought him bowls of soup. For a week we kept the fire going through the night.

"When finally he recovered, Jean-Pierre said he wanted to help us. If our baby was a girl, he would marry her when she turned sixteen," said Isabelle.

The tale of her engagement bewildered Sophie. Her childhood with André had vanished in an instant, for what meaning could it have, when another man had claimed her from the first? The times André had teased her and the times she had run to him had been like the stones they gathered on the beach to make castles.

With those moments she had still hoped to build a life with him.

But no longer.

When her mother had finished speaking, Sophie's face was as smooth as sand swept by a wind.

Several days later an elaborately dressed man appeared in the doorway of the Armants' cottage. He was wearing a bright orange waistcoat and his skin looked nearly blue against the garish color.

Sophie drew back.

Jean-Pierre Blanchard was as dismayed. One day, artists in their portraits of Sophie would calm her unruly curls and paint her rosy cheeks a fashionable cream. Their generous brush strokes would round her slight body. But Jean-Pierre saw her natural state. With her heightened color and her eager look, Sophie seemed to be leaning into a strong

March wind—or into the future, he thought. And yet, though he would complain of her thinness and her vivid face to his three pale, plump sisters, he would keep his promise to marry Sophie. For in this day of excesses of every sort, he had been praised for his romantic gesture to help a poor family.

Sophie took three bowls from the cupboard and put them on the table. Then she went back and got out another. Carefully she set a knife and spoon beside each one. Certainly Monsieur Blanchard was grateful to her parents for having taken him in, she thought, but there must be more to it than that. Her mother was curved where she was not. Watching Isabelle pour coffee into the bowls, Sophie wondered if all those years ago, Jean-Pierre Blanchard had fallen in love with young Madame Armant and, unable to have the mother, had decided to pledge himself to the unborn daughter and hope for the best.

That evening Sophie made her first entry in the copybook diary she would keep fitfully for years: "Maman says Monsieur Blanchard is an aeronaut, a famous one. He flies through the air in a basket."

Looking out the window at the night sky, she tried to imagine such a thing.

The next afternoon Sophie stood at the edge of the sea. In one hand she held a soup ladle and in the other the length of stiff cloth for her wedding dress. Her gray-striped cat sat on a rock nearby. Sophie knew the village superstition that if she stepped on its right front paw her marriage would be postponed for half a year. But she didn't want to try. Just as the night before she had said no when her mother suggested she go and live in Toulouse with friends.

Her family's plight was hers, and soon it would be hers to ease as well. Besides, it had been a childish dream that someday André would marry her. Months ago, he had kissed her, but in a final way, as if something was over that once had been.

Frowning at the cheap linen, not sure that saltwater softened cloth, Sophie began to fill a hollowed-out stone. Usually when she got to the beach she took off her wooden shoes, but today she kept them on. As water and sand spilled in them they grew heavy, and she moved clumsily, walking back and forth with her ladle. After soaking the linen for some time, she shook it out and spread it on the sand. Specks of cloth wet with salt crystals sparkled in the air, and ordinarily she would have tried to catch them, but today she was deep in thought, trying to work out how she would live with a man who wasn't André Giroux.

Sophie had been raised on a white bone of sand in a wind that came from the sea. She knew there was no stopping it. Every day she saw it fling clouds across the marsh and continue on its way. Now, as she watched a gust of wind sail her length of linen across the sand, she decided that she would love Jean-Pierre Blanchard, and that her love would keep on going, luminous as sea air, until it reached André.

Kicking off her shoes, Sophie ran after her cloth and

weighted it with stones. When the linen was finally dry, she was surprised; the sun had bleached it, and the saltwater had softened the weave enough to be able to fold it into pleats and tucks.

Her future lay before her, a length of pale linen unwavering as a salt path.

On her way home, at first Sophie didn't recognize the bright drops glistening on the young green shoots of grass. They looked like sea spray reddened by the setting sun. But beyond them, partly hidden in the marsh, she saw the body of a soldier. Her hands trembled as she knelt and loosened his high collar; putting her cheek on the blue wool, she listened for breath.

Then she started off for André's house.

From his doorway he watched his childhood friend flying unfurled along the salt paths. Sophie was awkward and inclined to stumble. As always, André wanted to go to her to catch her if she fell. Instead he waited until she ran up to him, flushed and out of breath, a thin arm thrown back against the wind. He wanted to draw her wide-eyed face to his. But he only straightened her shawl, which had loosened in her hurry. Then, as she told him about the fallen soldier and pointed across the marsh, in a rare gesture, he touched her outstretched hand.

Despite her worry, Sophie was shyly pleased.

A few minutes later sixteen-year-old André was examining the soldier's bloody arm. Probably the long, shallow cut had been made by a pitchfork. King Louis XVI had been beheaded the year before, but in the Vendée, the region north of La Salière, royalist peasants still fought republican soldiers with anything they had.

André placed his hands on the soldier's chest, and after some time he began to move and flail about. But as soon as he looked at André his breathing steadied. Finally he stood, and when André slipped the jacket around his shoulders, he started walking down the path, then stopped for a moment and glanced back, bewildered, startling Sophie with his light eyes.

But André waved him on.

What had occurred didn't seem remarkable to Sophie. For as long as she could remember, André had been healing their neighbors, doing the work of their bodies until they could take it up again. "How do you suppose he does it?" the villagers asked her when they were well. Sophie used to say it was the magic in André's hands. But one day he had talked to her about the people he tried to help, how they had lost hope or were afraid; and how sometimes he was the only one left who believed they could get well.

"If they learn to trust me, they lose their fear and try," he said, holding out nicked and calloused hands to show her there was no magic in them.

And so to the people who wanted to know, Sophie described the day André turned six and refused to put on his dress. Boys had to wait until they were nine or ten to wear long pants, but that morning his rage had been heard across the salt flats and he had never worn skirts again.

"André's will is strong enough to walk across," was Sophie's explanation.

Now she ran to gather up the linen cloth that had billowed across the marsh.

"What is all this for?" André asked as she folded it up and put it in her basket.

"My wedding dress."

It was all Sophie had time to say, for he had turned away.

When they set off for La Salière, a full moon was rising. The light on the crystalline paths was so bright the rest of the marsh was sunk in darkness, and they walked on white lines suspended in space. But despite the beauty of the night, Sophie was silent. André was often irritable after a cure, and she was sure it was because he was angry at being different from the other boys. Though it didn't stop him from losing himself—at his peril, it seemed to her—in trying to save what others couldn't.

That evening, over and over, Sophie called up the moment on the salt marsh when André had put his hand on hers. His touch had been warm and sure, with the clean smell of salt.

Neither of them gave a thought to the soldier slowly walking south, but Colonel Marc-Emmanuel Duroc was certain that the pair had saved his life.

⌒

2

A WEDDING IN LA SALIÈRE

EVEN IN FULL SPRING THE LANDSCAPE around La Salière changed little.

Few flowers could bloom in salt, and only small pink
roses were strong enough to push their way through close-
rooted marsh grasses. Still, June was a time for weddings.
Two weeks after his first visit Jean-Pierre Blanchard drew a
carriage up to the Armants' cottage. He was alone. Others
might praise him for his generous offer to marry Sophie, but
his three sisters considered it a madcap notion.

Even though everyone in La Salière attended the wedding,
the gathering was small. Most of the men were conscripted
into the army and only a few girls and boys Sophie's age still
lived in the village. The group fit easily into the mayor's office for the civil ceremony, the only kind allowed by the new
French republic.

As Sophie stood before them her back was straight. It was
a legacy from her mother.

Isabelle Armant never spoke of her childhood in a château beyond La Rochelle, but she had given her only daughter remnants of it. She had passed on the old family names and a bearing different from that of the other village girls. The night before, Isabelle had touched her daughter's face, the sight as necessary to her as breathing; soon something she must live without. Then she had drawn woven silver and gold ribbons from a box. "These were given to me on my wedding day," she said. "I wore them on my wedding cap and so will you."

In the mayor's office, as Sophie held her head high and said her vows, André Giroux saw her transformed beneath a bit of antique lace into a mystery beyond his reach. He watched their mothers—his and Sophie's—turn from each other in a slow flare of long black skirts. When he was younger, André had been confused when his mother and Madame Armant had exchanged complicit glances, but now he understood.

After the ceremony, the villagers walked to the Armants' cottage to eat the yellow cake Sophie's mother had made, but André didn't go to the wedding breakfast. He strode along a footpath on the coast until he reached a gold tidal pool. The water was clear, nearly transparent, and he could see the shadows of minnows flickering on the sandy bottom. He smiled for a moment, remembering that when she was a child, Sophie had thought fish flew through the air.

They had come here often.

Even when André was young his hands had held a man's gift, while Sophie's had held his childhood. He had been able to be a boy only with her. But as he grew older, sometimes the healing in his hands had been lost in his growing love for her. He worried that healing called for a heart committed to many, not just one, and so he had turned away from Sophie. Given time, he had hoped to learn how to honor both.

Shades of blue still darkened toward the middle of the pool where he and Sophie used to swim. André took aim. He hurled rock after rock into the deepest blue-brown water, roiling it up until the placid sunlit pool was torn apart.

Later, he stood in a shadowed doorway with his hands on his hips and watched Sophie dance across the village square toward him. The fiddler's tune was simple, like thread unwinding from a spool, and it drew her away from Jean-Pierre so lightly it seemed as if she had never been at his side.

In that moment no one was more graceful.

With her dark hair knotted sleekly on her neck Sophie turned as a dancer turns, and each step took her farther from Jean-Pierre. Astonished, the peasants saw her slight figure spin out of the pattern of the dance. The profile of her face, fine as cut crystal, turned toward them and then away.

Sophie seemed to be heeding something in the music, when suddenly the fiddler put down his bow.

Everyone was sure the old man's wrists had started to ache again, but that wasn't it. For a few wild moments with his fiddle he had tried to help André. Six years before, he hadn't been able to play a note, until the boy had healed him. As if it were yesterday, the fiddler remembered the stillness of André's gaze—its weight and heft. The boy had been ten years old then, already walking like a man, and the little one had run ahead along the salt paths. He had found them a perfect pair.

But it wasn't right to interfere, the old man thought, putting down his bow in the middle of his song. Sophie, startled, stopped dancing, then seeing André's eyes on her, looked down and touched the stiff ivory folds of her wedding gown.

After she and Jean-Pierre had raised glasses of *pineau,* they rode out of the village. Passing André on the road, Sophie couldn't know he had just decided to leave La Salière. She only knew that when he caught sight of her in the back window of the carriage, he scowled and looked away.

From the Atlantic coast, the road rose steadily upland toward Les Petits-Andelys, where Jean-Pierre had been born forty-two years before. The carriage rattled from side to side and tipped so on the twisting roads that Sophie was frightened. She had never traveled far from her village or climbed a hill, and their fitful progress, combined with the smell of horse sweat and fresh-dropped manure, made her sick.

Hours later they swayed down the valley to Jean-Pierre's village on a bank of the Seine. Long branches overhead formed a green tunnel filled with dark sweet forest smells. When Sophie and Jean-Pierre emerged for a moment or two, before the slap of a branch signaled another ride through murky yellow-green light, all she saw was more green—the green of mountains stretching up from the valley floor as high as she could see.

Sophie threw up as they circled around the church in Les Petits-Andelys and drew up to a large limestone house attached to others like it; on the front steps, Jean-Pierre's three sisters were gathered to greet them. Knowing smiles lighted their faces. Sophie's indisposition was only to be expected, the nerves of a young girl anticipating her wedding night. Fussing with wet cloths and tidying her grimy figure, they did their best to welcome the child bride of their adored brother.

But there came the moment when the family went to bed and the wedding couple tucked themselves under the eaves and into the silence of the tall white house. Jean-Pierre approached Sophie with misgivings. He was used to bodies that seemed to contain no bones. The atmosphere in his household was the floury softness of hands that had never pulled a salt rake or been cut on a mussel shell. In Les Petits-Andelys, peasant women bared their bosoms to feed the babies of elegant Parisians; though they plied their trade discreetly, it was obvious their breasts were big and soft as fresh loaves of bread, and Jean-Pierre had loved them since he was a boy.

By the standards of his fecund village, Sophie was thin as butcher's string. Lying on their marriage bed in her gauzy nightdress, she was barely embodied. Her small frame held out the promise of succulence, like a morsel of tender quail, but not to someone reared on abundance. As Jean-Pierre put his hands here and there, her knobby terrain became sadly apparent. Worse, he felt her heart, so lightly encased, beating as steadily as if she were bowed in prayer. Despite this he persevered.

But by the time he fell upon her little rib cage, Sophie's heart had lighted out for André.

CGG 3 G

HOUSEKEEPING

"MAMAN!" WAS SOPHIE'S ONE-WORD ENTRY in her diary the next morning.

When she came downstairs the Blanchard family was already at breakfast. They were talking about a new basket Jean-Pierre must see but fell silent when Sophie slid into the only chair left. For as soon as she sat down between two ample sisters, a third, her arms filled with hot fragrant croissants from the bakery across the square, walked in to find her seat taken.

A chair was quickly brought and another plate was laid as plump hands passed the warm rolls around the table and talk resumed about the special basket. But Sophie was uncomfortable. She was sorry she had taken someone's place and she couldn't understand why Jean-Pierre was interested in a picnic hamper. An hour later as they set out for a walk along the grassy bank of the Seine, she didn't like the gnats and flies that settled everywhere in the still air.

When Jean-Pierre opened a barn door there wasn't even

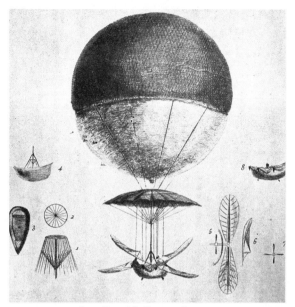

Jean-Pierre's Flying Airship

the pretty wicker basket she had been hoping to see but a huge wooden one with giant feathers coming out of the sides. He said it would fly, with a balloon attached. With hand pedals and foot pedals, he could agitate the feathers so that some would rise and others would fall, imitating the flight of birds. Sophie smiled politely but this struck her as a lunatic notion, and, when he said the balloon was made of varnished silk, dangerous as well. Such delicate fabric would keep no one in the air for long.

Jean-Pierre climbed into his blue basket.

Stirring his feathers into action, he spoke of the velocity of the balloon in terms of its quantity of action and its surface of resistance. Then he clambered back down and went over to his workbench, where he wrote this:

$$V = \sqrt[3]{\frac{2yfg\sqrt{b}}{a\phi(\sqrt{a} + \sqrt{b})}}$$

Sophie didn't understand, of course, but she found the lines and letters beautiful. They didn't wobble like her columns of addition. She examined them closely.

"Where are the feathers?"

"Here," said Jean-Pierre, pointing to the b. "The a is the surface of resistance."

"And the V is the velocity," Sophie said.

She wished he would show her more, but his excitement had given way to a more down-to-earth concern. Was there a wagon large enough in Les Petits-Andelys to transport the basket to Paris, where they were to live?

Sophie glanced back at the Seine, flat and green as pea soup in a bowl. She didn't like the bug-filled air above it, but anything was better than riding up and down the hills to Paris in a wagon with no sides.

"Perhaps you could put the basket on a barge," she suggested.

The Blanchards stared at Sophie. It hadn't occurred to them to appropriate the Seine. Jean-Pierre flushed—though whether from pride in his young wife's intelligence, or irritation that she had thought of it first, even his sisters couldn't tell.

For three days horses on the towpath pulled the barge steadily upriver. The current on the Seine was always slow from Les Petits-Andelys east to Paris, and the barge was steady as a house. But Sophie was unnerved. Standing on water that looked like thick soup was different from floating in a clear tidal pool that looked like air.

Though the bargeman's six children seemed to manage well enough. The oldest ones, Christian and Christiane, boasted of seeing the bore, a rogue wave on the west leg of the river that trawled walls of water sixteen feet high. And just this morning Sophie had nearly stumbled over the littlest ones—Bernard and Bernadette—curled up in coils of line. (When the bargeman picked them up, he had handed one to Sophie, saying, "Once you choose a name, you might as well get good use of it!")

The activity on the Seine stretched from one edge of Sophie's vision to the other. Châteaus, forests, backwaters, church towers, vineyards. Her eyes ached trying to keep track of it all. But no matter how long she looked, eventually everything ended up downstream and out of sight—the houseboat with its pots of red geraniums, the fisherman in his blue boat, and the children standing on the riverbank.

The changeless landscape of her childhood with its wide skies and endless ocean had not prepared Sophie for these disappearing acts on the Seine.

In La Salière, nothing had ever gone away.

Now she could only watch as the present seemed to float into the past, into the place where André was, and forever lost to view.

But for Jean-Pierre the river called up memories, and he smiled as they neared Freneuse. The village tailor had made the orange waistcoat he had worn in America, on his balloon flight from the nation's capital. He had been pleased when George Washington walked over to the courtyard of the old Philadelphia prison to see his balloon, though he had found the president's attire disappointing. Washington had worn a black velvet suit, the somber effect only moderately brightened by yellow gloves.

He frowned as they approached Sèvres. Beyond it, at the Palace of Versailles, a hundred thousand people had gathered in 1783 to watch the first balloon ascension—not his! The French revolution had been six years away when King Louis XVI arranged for the Paris Academy of Sciences to use its three-foot quadrant and measure the height the sphere attained. "It looks as if we're going all the way to heaven on wings of our own," American ambassador to France Thomas Jefferson had said, marveling at the magnificent azure sphere decorated with gold festoons and signs of the zodiac.

Jean-Pierre had been pacing the deck. Now he paused to ruminate in envy. The balloon's inventor, Étienne Montgolfier, was admired as much for his tranquility and understated attire as for the magnificence of his achievement. "There is no one more modest than Monsieur Montgolfier," the newspapers always said.

"Get out, get out!" yelled Jean-Pierre, seeing the third pair of barge children—Yves and Yvette—wrestle in his new blue basket. He glared at the littlest ones now asleep on white balloon silk.

Sophie was quiet for a moment. She knew she and André had napped like that as babies, cocooned together in a blanket on the beach while their mothers had gathered mussels. She had thought of him on the barge ride, when she saw children playing at the edge of the Seine, then watched them slip past her in the wake. But now she turned and looked toward Paris; like the crosscurrents on the river, along with the sorrow of leave-taking was anticipation at what was to come.

When Sophie and Jean-Pierre reached the city, other than women washing their families' clothes in the river, few people were about. But no sooner were they walking along the Left Bank than a mighty hymn rang out, for all of Paris had gathered to celebrate the Festival of the Supreme Being. Though Maximilien Robespierre—the president of the National Convention—made sure the chorus raised its voices in praise of the new French republic as well: on the Champ-de-Mars, on the plateaus and escarpments of an enormous plaster mountain constructed for the occasion, twenty-four hundred choristers sang "La Marseillaise."

Sophie stared at the faux mountain peak where a statue of a man clutched another, much smaller statue of freedom, and thought of the unfettered wind that had blown through her childhood. She gazed around her at the long breadlines and the young boys crisscrossing the Champ-de-Mars with pails of water hung from poles on their shoulders.

On their way to Jean-Pierre's apartment a woman walked up to them with an urn of café au lait strapped to her back. Jean-Pierre poured some into two earthenware bowls but poured it back when she told him it cost four sous. A few minutes later, when he unlocked the door at 20, rue Cassette, Sophie understood why he was so careful with his money.

The rooms were large, which meant he had once been rich, but the walls were sooty and the gilt moldings were crumbling, which meant he wasn't now.

In the weeks that followed, Sophie was often alone, for Jean-Pierre was absorbed in reestablishing his aeronautical career. He had spent several years in America, where he had ascended only once, in Philadelphia, and had returned to France just recently. Sophie spent the days exploring Paris, and one morning in the Luxembourg Gardens she stopped to watch a blacksmith work the bellows and hammer hot steel into a gun barrel.

At makeshift foundries all over the city, workmen were melting down church bells and metal statues of the Virgin Mary and turning out seven hundred rifles a day. The fighting in the Vendée was making insatiable demands of a nation reeling from years of hunger and death, and now the new republic had declared war on Austria as well.

Women sewing uniforms and tents glanced up at Sophie. The girl was runty. From the look of her she was used to fancy needlepoint.

"I can sew a hem," Sophie said.

A woman in a dirty dress grabbed her hand and felt for the callous from sewing with no thimble. She stared at Sophie in surprise. "The girl will do. But give her wool, not canvas."

Stitching the rough cloth reminded Sophie of her coarse linen wedding dress. She wondered for a moment what might have happened if she had kept dancing across the square until she reached André. The thought was small but disturbing, like a drop of water in a still pool, and she pulled too hard on her needle. The thread snapped, and the women frowned as the jacket sleeve slipped from Sophie's lap.

She was bent over her sewing again when crowds surged through the Luxembourg Gardens. Putting down his bellows, a smithy walked over to the women to tell them Robespierre had just been guillotined, along with twenty-two others. Mostly they were those whose livelihoods depended on the favors of the rich, wigmakers and chocolate makers, dancing masters and the like. People were complaining of the blood running in the streets.

It was some time before Sophie's hands stopped shaking and she could sew.

That afternoon when she came home she watched Jean-Pierre dig up saltpeter in the cellar and put a basketful on the steps outside. She knew it would be picked up and made into gunpowder. Sophie walked into his workroom. Surely there was some small thing she could set against the threat of violence that was everywhere, now even on their own doorstep. Opening the doors of an armoire, she studied the bright balloon silks piled on the shelves.

CÆ 4 ßD

TWO SOLDIERS
FROM BRIENNE

TWELVE DAYS AFTER ROBESPIERRE'S DEATH, high above Nice in a fort overlooking the turquoise blue Bay of Antibes, the young republican soldier Napoleone Buonaparte was imprisoned for being a friend of Robespierre's brother.

Napoleone didn't understand.

"First it's republicans against royalists and now it's republicans against republicans," he complained to an old friend from military school, now a soldier like himself. "What's next?"

"Republicans against tyrants," said Colonel Marc-Emmanuel Duroc, unbuttoning the collar of his blue uniform. "The new republic's decided to help *every*body overthrow their rulers."

"*That's* more like it!" Napoleone said.

Marc-Emmanuel grinned. It had been some time since he had heard those rolling *r*'s. As boys at military school in Brienne, they had quarreled over whether Corsica was French or Italian. Napoleone Buonaparte hadn't wanted his native island occupied by France, but at the same time he had seemed to want to be French.

"I brought those histories you asked for," said Marc-Emmanuel. With his friend under lock and key, at least this time there was a chance of getting his books back. Buonaparte always read as he rode at the head of a column, and when he finished a page he tore it out and threw it away.

The August day was hot and Marc-Emmanuel took off his wool jacket. Rolling up a sleeve, he pointed to a long, narrow scar. "It was the damnedest thing. There was this girl and boy, I swear they saved my life, and I'm going to find them—"

Marc-Emmanuel stopped. Napoleone wouldn't be interested in his plan. He was already reading, and scarcely looked up to say good-bye.

In La Salière a few days later, an old man guided Marc-Emmanuel to the Armant cottage.

Watching Sophie's mother move gracefully around the fire preparing tea, he had the feeling she was playing a part. She seemed to wear her heavy peasant skirt as if it were a costume. Marc-Emmanuel thought the shelves of books looked out of place as well; so many in a peasant cottage was unusual.

But that impression was quickly replaced by another. As he listened to her brief replies to his questions about her daughter and the young healer, Marc-Emmanuel found Madame Armant voluptuous, and all the more seductive for her reticence and her slender ankles anchored in wooden shoes. It was the beginning of his years-long dream—a quiet fire and evenings spent reading aloud to Isabelle Armant.

The next afternoon Marc-Emmanuel found himself in a church in La Rochelle, at first amused by the women clustered around the handsome young healer, then intrigued as André passed his hands across the unblinking gaze of a little boy. The child flinched when a man—Marc-Emmanuel assumed him to be the father—stepped forward. André moved so that he was between father and son. He murmured, and Marc-Emmanuel saw the boy's black eyes fasten on the healer.

But when André led him back to his father, the child was unseeing.

"What did you say to the boy?" Marc-Emmanuel asked later as they sat outside at a café.

"I told him that if he could see, he could run," said André, taking a sip of Cognac.

"Do you think he will see again?" said Marc-Emmanuel.

"He might. He wasn't afraid of me. Which means he isn't frightened yet of everyone."

There was a slap on André's shoulder.

"Miche," he said, not looking up. "How goes it?"

"No complaints." Another slap and the man had gone.

"He's in charge of conscripting soldiers in my district," said André. "He won't let me sign up."

"You're crazy!" said Marc-Emmanuel. "You're too young to go. Besides, you can do more for France here in La Rochelle, and stay alive in the bargain!"

André set his jaw. "I *will* go someday, when Miche is off the job."

As an officer assigned to the new government in Paris, Marc-Emmanuel could have helped André. Instead he said, "I'm on my way to Paris. Do you have a message for Sophie?" He saw André's face brighten for a moment, but the boy shook his head.

"None."

Marc-Emmanuel thought nothing of it. He had just decided that the young man who had saved his life needed looking after himself. As a cold wind began to wash over the quai, he invited André to join him for supper.

Already that December there had been days of record cold in Paris. As Marc-Emmanuel rode through the Bois de Boulogne he saw gangs of women and children ranging though the forest and chopping wood.

He reined in his horse at 20, rue Cassette, and knocked.

"I remember your light eyes," said young Madame Blanchard.

When they had climbed the stairs and were standing in her salon, Marc-Emmanuel glanced hungrily at her slender form, hoping for signs of her mother. But Madame Blanchard was as fragile as the wisps of colorful silk pinned to the walls. Marc-Emmanuel smiled. He was descended from an old Beaune family with a château decorated with gold leaf and family portraits. Here spread out on a writing table—the only proper piece of furniture in the room—were drawings of feathers and spheres, and sketches of contraptions with pedals and what looked like oars. But despite the salon's bohemian charm and exotic aeronautical touches, Madame

Blanchard's concerns seemed ordinary enough. She said that in the months since her marriage her husband was often away, traveling to the cities and villages that paid him to ascend in their festivals. He was in Bordeaux and wouldn't be home for another week.

In turn Marc-Emmanuel told her about his life before the revolution when his family had gathered in their chapel for midnight Mass. Then he mentioned seeing André in a church in La Rochelle and noticed her face shine briefly, but she offered tea as if she hadn't heard. "Frankly, I thought the women were a little in love with André," Marc-Emmanuel added. "I am not sure they all needed healing."

Sophie was busy with the teapot and didn't look up.

Over the next weeks and months, because of Jean-Pierre's frequent absences, Marc-Emmanuel fell into the habit of dropping in to see Sophie; as with André, he felt a need to look after her. One morning, out walking in a chill rain, he and Sophie passed men and women warming themselves at open fires, and Marc-Emmanuel took her arm. He knew she was likely to tremble, just as he knew she would reach for sous in the bright silk pocket she had sewn on her skirt.

Sophie was talking about the night she and her mother had sat outside in a dark summer wind and counted fireflies until they had fallen asleep in the marshgrass. Although the story appealed greatly to Marc-Emmanuel, he stopped her and waved to a thin figure walking slowly toward them down the rainy allée.

"Buonaparte! I haven't seen you since they let you out of prison!"

Most likely it was the rain that made the soldier's hair so lank, Sophie thought. The cuffs on his coat were frayed, and his boots were cracked as well as muddy. He must be very poor, she decided, as Marc-Emmanuel held her arm firmly to discourage her tremor and introduced her to Napoleone Buonaparte.

Who gazed at young Madame Blanchard for a long moment, then mumbled a few words and continued on his way.

"We fought together when he captured Toulon," Marc-Emmanuel explained. "Think of it, Napoleone went into that battle a captain and came out a brigadier general. And then, when Robespierre was guillotined, he was thrown in jail. Small wonder nobody understands what's going on in France!"

"They say he's lying low in the Latin Quarter without a sou to his name."

Napoleone's gait was uneven as he passed the busts of ancient Roman heroes that lined the walk. "Just look at him," said Marc-Emmanuel. "There's a general in Toulon says he can't understand why the little bastard frightens him so. I swear I can't either."

A few minutes later in a hotel on rue de la Huchette, in a large tidy room where two young soldiers sprawled on their beds, Brigadier General Buonaparte stood bareheaded before the fire. He was cold, but then he always was.

Walking into his room, he frowned at his messy sheets and the litter of books. Here he was, a military hero, and he

couldn't afford wood or hot water or a maid! He'd been better off at military school. There they had given him five-
course dinners and wine to boot. Though he'd complained
even then that poor boys like him were getting used to a life
they hadn't a prayer of maintaining. And he was right, wasn't
he? His hat was hanging at Le Procope as security until he
could pay his wine bill!

Worse, no letter had come.

In silence Marmont handed him a hot, wet cloth but
Junot couldn't resist. "She's not even pretty! Forget her!" But
Napoleone loved sweet, innocent Desirée Clary. These days,
he was tempted to step in front of an approaching carriage,
and he was sure it was for lack of a letter from her and not
because of his uncertain future.

Even though, in the novel he had just finished reading for
the seventh time, the melancholy of Goethe's young hero was
caused as much by ambition as by love.

That afternoon thousands of royalists rose up. They shouted
and shoved their way along the Left Bank and across the
Pont Neuf. At midnight, joined by crowds of penniless republicans, they marched on the government offices. The
head of the republic's forces, General Paul Barras, was hard
pressed to find a seasoned artilleryman, but he had seen
Buonaparte a day or two before. At Toulon the young
brigadier general had refused to leave his post and had slept
on the ground in his overcoat.

Hours later, as women converged on the Tuileries Gardens shouting "Peace!" a lean young man in an old gray coat

quelled the uprising by ordering cannon fire and killing fourteen hundred Parisians. Afterward, everyone said it had been a ruthless decision to fire into the crowd, it had never been done before; but some republicans added that it had saved France from more Bourbon kings.

By nightfall Napoleone Buonaparte had been promoted and the name of the penniless twenty-six-year-old Sophie had just met was known all over Paris.

5

THREADS

THE AIR WAS THICK with flying yellow leaves the day that fall when Sophie and Jean-Pierre rode through the beech forests to Lyon. There had been no gold trees in La Salière and Sophie was on her way to her first balloon ascension, but even excitement couldn't lessen her fear of riding in a carriage.

After she and Jean-Pierre had driven onto a cobbled square and the wagons loaded with equipment had pulled in, the area was roped off, for tickets were sold to those who wanted to come near the airship; the rest of Jean-Pierre's earnings would come from the fee Lyon paid him to ascend.

Sophie watched the handlers hauling off heavy tanks. When Jean-Pierre said each one contained a hundred pounds of sulfuric acid, she began to count. Half an hour later, she told him that four thousand four hundred pounds of acid had been taken off the wagons, and Jean-Pierre nodded. "The oak barrels are filled with the same weight in iron filings. Together they make hydrogen."

MAKING HYDROGEN

Next the basket was unloaded, as well as the smaller gear—sandbags, filters, anchor, restraining cord, iron stakes, and the like. The balloon itself had been made in Lyon and arrived on a wagon half an hour later. Unfolded, the empty yellow bag was eighty feet long, nearly the length of the square.

Even before the unpacking was completed, two men were diluting the sulfuric acid and pouring it over iron filings. As soon as the acid stopped bubbling they reactivated it with more filings so that gas was kept flowing up through the filter and into the balloon. Carefully, a workman swabbed the lower part of the balloon with water. "The acid reaction makes it hot," he told Sophie. "But even if only a drop of water enters the balloon, sulfuric acid forms instead of gas, and it eats through the lining."

A few hours later Sophie was dumbfounded. The balloon was made of nearly nothing at all, thin silk filled with a gas that didn't weigh an ounce, yet now it was taller than the tallest house! The sphere sat like an immense gold sun behind a tangle of wrought iron gates and cobbled streets then rose majestically far above the Saône and Rhône rivers and the staircase-towers of Lyon. But despite the balloon's stately air, Sophie noticed that people smiled when they looked at it, as they wouldn't at a carriage or a ship.

That evening on place de la Baleine, Lyon's prettiest square, the silk manufacturer Cusset stood in his doorway to greet Madame and Monsieur Blanchard. Most of his time was spent at his Paris shop but he had come to his factory in Lyon to supervise the construction of Blanchard's balloon and witness the flight. In Cusset's seventeenth-century house the Aubusson rugs were pale, the Riesener furniture distinguished. He and the Blanchards were to dine on quenelles in a crayfish sauce followed by capon stuffed with truffles, and hazelnut tortes. The service, despite the ornate silver and fragile sèvres, would be soundless.

"It was splendid to see my gold silk flying through the sky," Cusset told the aeronaut. "Draped in a salon or a theater is one thing. Decorating the heavens is quite another, *non*?"

The silk maker turned next to Madame Blanchard, gleaming in a cream-colored gown. He saw that she had lined the pleats of her skirt with scraps of his silks in shades of cerise, azure, cinnabar, emerald, and magenta. Silk owes its brilliance to an unusual capacity for absorption, but Cusset's dyeing techniques produced particularly jewel-like tones.

"Madame, you honor me. I recognize my work here as well, do I not?"

"You do, monsieur. Your silks shine like no others."

The pleats shimmered when she moved.

"Hand-loomed silk is the most beautiful," said Cusset. "As much because of its imperfections as its sheen." Just as Madame Blanchard's appeal lies in her small flaws, he thought. The tiny mole at the corner of her left eye. The front tooth set at a charming angle.

"But all silks are strong," he continued. "The filaments come originally from the same eggs—we call them silk seeds—smuggled out of China in hollow bamboo canes a thousand years ago. The best and strongest silk is made when two worms nest together in a single cocoon. Their threads aren't separated and so the filament is doubly strong. As strong as steel."

The silk maker was struck by Madame Blanchard's sudden radiance, for the light in her face outshone the candles.

From the time she and André had been swaddled together on the beach, Sophie thought, they had seen with each other's eyes as well as their own. The same strand of memories had united them, and she wondered if, like a doubled thread, it might have made their love stronger.

Sophie's smile lasted only a moment, but it was long enough for Cusset to remark upon her beauty. Often he speculated about what rendered a length of cloth especially striking. Certainly silkworms were sensitive creatures—perhaps excessively so. Every silk maker knew they refused to feast on faded leaves and liked them fresh and green—though slightly wilted. Still, no one could say why some worms produced threads that wound up so startlingly turquoise or so startlingly cerise. But Cusset had no need to deliberate over Madame Blanchard's beauty. There was her luminous face tinged just now with cerise, his favorite silk dye. And there was her straight back with its shoulder wings sharp like a child's. What did it matter, which of these made her unforgettable?

It occurred to the silk maker that Sophie Blanchard was still young and not yet fully formed. She seemed to have an expectant air, and he wondered what her life would bring. "Silkworms release a fluid that hardens into silk," Cusset told her. "They wind it around themselves to make a cocoon, and wait inside until their wings have grown and they can fly."

⌒

ᑕᘓ 6 ᘒᑐ

SALT

DURING HER LONG WALKS ALONE Sophie thought of André, and one day she found a corner of Paris that reminded her of him.

It was the gravel courtyard of the Luxembourg Palace.

She had still been small when André had handed her a salt rake, saying, "Your father isn't well and your mother can't do this alone." He hadn't laughed when she tried to wield the handle two feet taller than she, only put his hands on hers and showed her how to bring it forward, then draw it back. "Like the pendulum on your mother's clock," he said. "Swinging makes it easier."

Salt had stung the cuts on Sophie's hands and made her cry. But in time callouses had replaced the blisters and she grew to love the work. She would fling the heavy rake skyward, then bend and draw it in hand over hand. She became lithe and quick, and learned to judge when to begin the next swing up to the sky by the speed of the rake's pull toward her. Years later her neighbors told her she had been a gallant sight—"The work so hard and you so small!"

Sophie and André had worked together until a fall afternoon when they were fourteen. The wind was cold and it began to rain. Sophie had untied her shawl and wrapped it around them both. Their rakes bumping over the salt flats, they had run home laughing through the pelting rain, but suddenly André's face had darkened and he had pulled away. Taking her rake, he had walked ahead of her so quickly that when she turned up the path, the rake was propped against her door and he was gone.

After that, André had joined her only rarely.

Now, in the gravel courtyard as she watched a workman swing the handle forward and let the rhythm take it, Sophie realized she had learned another lesson in her hours raking alone, that work could be a respite from pain. She envied the workman with his worn rake.

In Paris, she had nothing to put a hand to.

～

❧ 7 ☙

COURTSHIP CORSICAN STYLE

ONE DAY THAT FALL Napoleone went to his first victims' ball.

Only republicans who had been imprisoned were invited to these frenzied affairs, where women piled their hair high and tied red ribbons around their necks to mimic the work of the guillotine. They wore little, for often it had been shed earlier, but what they *had* put on was red. And then they danced all night. They danced everywhere, even on the tops of the tombs in the cemetery of St. Sulpice. At times they danced desperately, as if possessed. In a kind of exorcism, jerking their heads up and down, then up and down again, they mimicked the action of the guillotine.

And the next day they threw away their new satin slippers because they had worn them out.

Among the guests invited one evening was the woman Napoleone—and therefore history—would call Joséphine. Born on the island of Martinique, she had come to Paris and at sixteen she had married the aristocrat Alexandre de Beauharnais. He had been assigned a military post, but after his army was defeated, he had been put in prison and beheaded.

Joséphine de Beauharnais had also been imprisoned, and had nearly been guillotined. A hero of the revolution, General Lazare Hoche, had been in the same prison. Now she slept with him and on alternate nights with General Paul Barras.

But tonight in her cap of curls—cut short to honor those whose hair had been shorn to expose their neck to the blade—she put on a bright red dress and a new pair of dancing slippers. Then she tied a scarlet ribbon around her neck and went to the victims' ball.

Joséphine knew how to please a military man.

"What weapons do you fear, sir?" she asked a young soldier.

"Fans, madame," said Major General Buonaparte. He was succinct because he could think of nothing more to say. Though eager to join Joséphine's roster of bedfellows, when it came to courtship, he still had mud on his boots.

Several days later, Napoleone was calling on Joséphine for the second time. Dinner the day before had gone badly. They had been alone and his impenetrable silence had fogged them in, had even seemed to dull the shine on the glass cabinets. He knew he lacked lightness and was inclined to be prudish; the scantily dressed women at the victims' ball had unnerved him. Suddenly Napoleone thought of his friend François Talma. Surely the best actor in France could teach him the role of the proper suitor!

Within an hour Talma was searching among his friend's blunt gestures for some unexpected gentleness he could turn to advantage. He was quickly discouraged. The man lacked polish and seemed to bark. Perhaps Napoleone should be taught to write of love, not speak of it.

The actor sighed. Of necessity, they would work through the night.

Early that evening as Sophie was walking home along rue des Capucines, she saw people gathered outside a window.

They were watching what looked like a play going on.

Two men stood close together, but the taller one was toying with an imaginary fan, and seemed to be acting the part of a woman. The small man bowed, but apparently it didn't suit the tall lady. The bow must have been too high, for the short man tried to bend lower, but couldn't. He shouted, and together they rushed to a table where, as the tall lady spoke, the small man wrote. Then, seeing the crowd of onlookers, he threw down his pen and hauled on the curtain as if the act was over.

Everyone clapped and laughed, talking about the actor Talma and wondering who the other man was. "Napoleone Buonaparte," said Sophie.

As time went by Napoleone made progress, though his friends couldn't understand it. Granted, at least he had lost interest in nondescript Desirée Clary. But Joséphine was nearly as unsuitable with her yellow teeth and big feet— thirty-three years to his twenty-seven! Besides, everybody knew that when Paul Barras wasn't waging war he was indulging Joséphine de Beauharnais's every sexual whim. His house surrounded by lilacs was a perfect copy of an unpretentious farmhouse, but it was common knowledge that beneath its simple thatched roof he conducted scenes of stunning debauchery. So everybody was surprised one evening to learn that Joséphine had been waiting in a local mayor's office since seven o'clock for Napoleone Buonaparte. She was sitting there with her old lover Barras and her friend Thérèse Tallien, watching a candle burn down to a nub.

When Buonaparte finally arrived from his office, three hours late, Joséphine looked down at the gold and silver medallion he had given her. *To Destiny* were the words engraved on it. She smiled. Well, that was why she had decided to marry him, after all. Everybody said Buonaparte was the coming man!

Within weeks of his wedding, Napoleone was on his way to Italy. Riding at the head of an army, he held a history of Egypt borrowed from Duroc, and one after another he ripped the pages out. The cavalrymen enjoyed the sport of spearing them, and after reading bits about pharaohs and pyramids they tossed the pages to the men farther back in line.

France's field guns were the best and lightest in Europe, and with them Napoleone intended to push the Austrians east and plunder Italy. Ordinarily it took three years to become an artillery officer but he had accomplished the task in six months; his plan for taking Italy was as efficient, the organization as intense. Among other things, he had calculated to within ten minutes where his regiments would camp at the end of each day.

"I am like a woman in labor," said Napoleone.

He was ready to take Italy, but first he removed an *e* from his first name and a *u* from his last, to make them look more French.

"Receive us with trust," General Napoleon Bonaparte told the Italian people as he emptied their boot. "Our only quarrel is with the tyrants who have enslaved us."

Privately he called Europe a molehill.

And looked farther south.

Meanwhile, "I send you a million kisses," he wrote to his wife. "I feel from your lips, your heart, a flame that consumes me." But François Talma had released a poet in the soldier to no avail. Just weeks after her marriage Joséphine had begun a passionate affair with the young army captain Louis-Hippolyte Quentin Charles. For two years no one would say a word about it to Napoleon. "I kiss your heart, and then a little lower," he wrote. "And then much lower still."

8

A SMALL WICKER BASKET

"I FEEL AS IF I'M LIVING ON the beach!" Jean-Pierre complained early one morning.

Sophie had had the ceilings of their apartment painted the color of a pale spring sky, and where they met the walls she had hung swags of silk in shades of gray to create the illusion of clouds. But just the impression of being in the open air—possibly at great height—distressed Jean-Pierre. The casement windows were open and the fabric billowed. Within its folds the silk darkened ominously.

"It's the same as sleeping outside!" he shouted.

Sophie walked in and shut the windows. "Now, now, chéri," she said gently. "You know it's only silk." Jean-Pierre was always upset before a flight, and that day he was to ascend for the first time in a closed basket. "I'm hoping it will make me feel as if I'm riding down a city street, not flying through the air," he had said. At first she had wondered why he continued to ascend when he was afraid, but then she realized that his wish for glory was greater even than his fear.

Marc-Emmanuel was to accompany Sophie and Jean-Pierre to Lieurey, where the ascension was to take place. They had arranged to meet that morning in Jean-Pierre's barn. While she waited, Sophie climbed into the blue basket with feathered oars she had seen in Les Petits-Andelys, but her legs weren't long enough to reach the foot pedals. Next to it, decorated with angels blowing trumpets, was a basket so large that sitting in it felt like being in a wagon.

In the back of the barn were piles of discarded balloon silks and basket linings. After rummaging through them Sophie lifted an old sheet lying in a corner.

Beneath it stood a small basket.

Even at each gently rising end it scarcely reached her hip.

The white canvas lining was spotless, though the wicker was honeyed with age.

Sitting in a shaft of sunlight, the basket nearly glowed.

"My second one," said Jean-Pierre, coming over for a look. "I've never used it because the workmen got the specifications wrong."

Sophie thought it was perfect. Usually the paraphernalia involved in flight was ponderous and complicated, but this little basket was so simple and elegant!

"Come along, it's time we got started," Jean-Pierre said impatiently. "Marc-Emmanuel is waiting in the wagon."

As she turned to leave, Sophie knocked a box off a table and hundreds of small brass grommets spilled to the floor.

"You clumsy colt!" shouted Jean-Pierre.

. . .

The December sun was bright that afternoon as ten-year-old
Louis Daguerre spun cartwheels down the Cormeilles hills.
A few minutes later he picked a leaf and flattened it on a
piece of vellum he tore from his sketchpad. After amusing
himself by making shadows on the pad with his hands, of a
lion roaring and a rooster crowing, he took out his pen and
began to draw. When he looked up, his eyes grew round at
the sight of the magnificent red sphere coming into view. As
soon as the balloon dipped behind a hill, the boy began to
run. He had been born in the Cormeilles hills and knew just
where to go. By the time he reached the valley the basket had
landed. Then a wagon pulled in and soon a few people were
clustered around.

Flipping his legs in the air, young Daguerre laughed out
loud as he walked over to them through the dried grasses on
his hands.

An hour later, waving good-bye to his new friends, he ran
back up the hill to get his things. Before he set off for home,
Daguerre lifted the leaf from the vellum, then stared at its
faint shadow fixed on the sun-bleached surface.

Early that evening Napoleon entered Paris after his victory in
Italy.

His horses were proceeding at a triumphal pace down rue
St. Honoré just as Jean-Pierre's wagon was crossing on his way
up rue de la Révolution. Marc-Emmanuel sat in the back,
leaning against the basket and waving to Napoleon, while
Sophie lay on the collapsed balloon, as Jean-Pierre had in-

structed, to keep it from sliding off. She looked pretty reflected in the glow of the balloon's rosy stripes. Shadowed by
a directional feather, her face appeared to be wreathed in
smiles. Napoleon was so taken by the sight of the beautiful
girl relaxing on a pile of red silk that, too late, he remembered his old friend.

The wagon had rattled past.

Actually Sophie wasn't smiling but grimacing. She hoped
she was sick because she was pregnant and not because of
the lurching wagon, for she was counting on a baby to open
a mother's heart to its father. But by the time they had
reached the barn and unpacked the balloon gear she felt as fit
as ever, and invited Marc-Emmanuel home for supper.

⌒

9

CONQUERING HERO

IT TOOK MONTHS FOR NAPOLEON to convince the French government that Egypt would make an excellent base for taking India from the British; and more months to plan the massive campaign. But finally he set out with four hundred ships and thirty-eight thousand soldiers. Accompanying them were twenty-one mathematicians, seventeen civil engineers, fifteen interpreters, four architects, three astronomers, a sculptor, a poet, a flower painter, and a musician or two; after his victory, Napoleon intended to settle a permanent colony in Egypt.

On the way (and spite of carrying the contents and population of a medium-sized city) he paused to reorganize Malta. It took him less than a week to abolish slavery and the nobility, structure the university system, and map the roads.

Then Napoleon sailed on and conquered Egypt. He had planned on staying until the work was going smoothly, but a chance remark helped him decide to sail home; though he was not absolutely certain Joséphine was having an affair with Louis-Hippolyte Quentin Charles.

"*You* would not go so far as to appropriate the wife of the conqueror of Egypt, would you?" he asked Marc-Emmanuel's cousin Christophe Duroc.

"*Non, non,*" said Duroc loyally. "Though others would. And do."

Napoleon longed to confront his wife, but his situation was complicated. The English had destroyed his navy, he was stranded in the desert, and his name was anathema among his troops. Despite this, claiming he left the Nile more beautiful than it had been for fifty years, Napoleon turned over his Egyptian command to General Paul Kléber and set sail to France.

In fact, behind him lay burned villages, an empty treasury, and an army decimated by battle and surrounded by a hostile population, as well as hundreds of ships gathering coral on the bottom of the sea.

After a six-week voyage, ordinarily the orange hills of Provence rising above Fréjus were an inviting sight to a Frenchman.

But not to Napoleon. Despite the seasickness that always confined him to his cabin, when he dropped anchor he put off going ashore. He was loath to face his countrymen. Not only had he lost their navy but he had also lost two-thirds of the soldiers they had entrusted to his command.

Why, he could hear the shouts even before he saw the crowds at the edge of the sea!

But to Napoleon's astonishment, instead of calumny there was praise, for the citizens of France needed a leader more than they needed the truth.

The members of the French government needed a leader too. But because of all the dancing in the streets, they didn't dare fire the man—despite his dismal failure in Egypt—who commanded the army of France. Even in the smallest villages torches lighted Napoleon's way north to Paris, where, in spite of a hero's welcome, the conqueror of Egypt came home to an empty house.

Joséphine had tried to meet him but mistook his route.

Now, weeping and pounding on the bedroom door, she stood in the hall and begged forgiveness for this as well as for her affair with Louis-Hippolyte Quentin Charles. Napoleon scarcely heard her through the thick panels. "I want a divorce!" he shouted, among many other things. But then he realized that the door muffled his blistering diatribe just as effectively as her pleas. He grew angrier and hollered for his brother Joseph, who hollered back that his career was finished if he and Joséphine divorced.

And so, after three days of this, though the doting husband was no more, Napoleon, wrapped in a white dressing gown with a madras handkerchief on his head, finally unlocked the bedroom door.

A few weeks later rain fell with little effect on the cobblestones of rue de la Roquette, but inside a shop the dampness expanded the dried herbs hanging from the ceiling and they unfolded their fragrances like fans. In this small room where no sunlight entered, the scent of a hundred mingling herbs reminded Sophie of her mother.

The herbalist considered why a healthy girl might be childless. Reaching up, she plucked a few leaves to restore the system's balance, and was adding a supply of a dried root to increase desire when another customer entered the shop.

"And so, success?" the herbalist asked the woman, whom she knew.

Making a pretty moue, the woman shook her head. She was holding a small packet. "My husband just brought this home from a trip. He was told it would help my condition, but we don't know what it is."

The herbalist tasted the powder. "Ashwagandha. An Indian herb, the root of the winter cherry. Very bitter but it might do some good."

What could be the problem? Sophie wondered. The lady's teeth were a little yellow, but surely she was in good health for she was dressed lightly despite the chill. In fact, she seemed to be wearing nearly nothing at all, her dress was so sheer.

"I suspect we share the same difficulty," the woman said to Sophie as she glanced at the herbs on the table. She smiled charmingly. "Permit me to give you a dose or two."

"With pleasure," Sophie said.

"I've thought of something!" the herbalist said as the women walked to the door. "A healer in La Rochelle is achieving remarkable cures. I have a friend who had bad gout—imagine, a Frenchman suffering from too much goose fat!—but no longer. The handsome young fellow works wonders—" She stopped, struck by the look on the girl's face.

It was like sunlight breaking through a cloud.

The other woman smiled and shrugged. "Perhaps," she said. "If my husband's ashwagandha is without effect. Au revoir, madame."

The women returned to the street and then to their separate beds, where after drinking his coffee, Jean-Pierre's first thought wasn't his usual disappointment in his wife's skimpy body. Sophie's heart, fortified by a tisane of false unicorn root and Napoleon's ashwagandha, flew to André more slowly than was usual. And in her dressing room lined with mirrors, Joséphine armed herself with the herbal gift from Egypt while Napoleon, like Jean-Pierre made less critical by a shot of saw palmetto, surrendered himself to a wife who had more lovers than he could count.

In spite of these efforts, no baby would issue from either bed.

Though admittedly, one room contained more than the usual worries. Napoleon was involved in plans for a coup d'état, and that night he was studying a book on how to read character in men's faces. When he finally blew out the candle, he counted up the number of generals on his side. "By the way," he said casually to Joséphine "tomorrow night we sleep in the Luxembourg Palace."

The next afternoon, he decided that on the way, he would have supper in the Church of St. Sulpice. It had been converted into a restaurant during the revolution, but Napoleon was afraid of being poisoned so he wrapped up a pear, some bread, and a bottle of Chambertin and brought them along.

The two towers of St. Sulpice functioned as a semaphore station.

While Napoleon sipped his wine, two men in each tower were relaying the news of his coup d'état by shutter flag to other stations, where they were received by telescope and sent on in a chain of messages that would reach Lyon in four hours and Strasbourg in six. Napoleon cocked his head, then smiled. By his count, five men were now in the towers. After years of silence, church bells had been recast and some were back in place. The fifth man was tolling the tocsin as the news of his victory swept France.

INTIMATIONS OF FLIGHT

IT WAS THE YEAR 1800, the dawn of a brand-new century, and Jean-Pierre was planning to take his wife to the city's first panorama. All of Paris was looking forward to it, but no one knew what it was. A round painting big enough to seat hundreds? No matter. Jean-Pierre had bought Sophie a dress for the occasion and she had just tried it on. He had to admit that in her orange taffeta, his wife was the very picture of an accomplished young Parisian matron.

Though he knew better. Sophie was afraid of everything and unable to bear him a child; after several years of marriage, she still gave away most of her coins before she reached the market. And she hadn't made a home worthy of a famous aeronaut, but something that looked like the beach in La Salière!

Now, while he was no admirer of Napoleon, ever since the Egyptian campaign tented rooms were all the rage in Paris, and even he had seen possibilities in the idea. A few weeks ago he had ordered lengths of silk and told his workmen to

JEAN-PIERRE CROSSING THE ENGLISH CHANNEL

stitch a narrow pocket down each strip before sewing them together; when the time came for the installation they slipped long curved wires inside.

The effect was so much more stylish than a military tent!

Jean-Pierre smiled as he sat inside the blue balloon that filled his salon.

Then he turned to preparing an article about his historic 1785 flight with an American doctor across the English Channel. Another balloonist had also wanted to be the first to cross, but though Pilâtre de Rozier had tried to frighten Jean-Pierre out of flying, it was de Rozier who had died in the attempt.

Jean-Pierre paused. People had loved de Rozier as they didn't love him, probably because the fellow's lectures had been full of jokes and tricks. There had been no need for de Rozier to take in a bit of hydrogen gas, then put a candle to his mouth and breathe out violet fire. He could perfectly well have filled a beaker and lighted that! "It is said that perhaps he loved glory too much," one eulogist wrote after de Rozier's death over the Channel in hydrogen's violet flames. "Ah! How could one be French and not love it?"

How indeed! Jean-Pierre thought as he sharpened his quill.

Sophie squirmed on the gold-embroidered daybed. In her stiff dress, she felt as bound up as an Egyptian mummy. Her shoulders itched.

"I want to fly," she said. As a tired child might, to test the way it sounded.

And observe its effect.

Jean-Pierre looked up. Sophie had kicked off her slippers and was pulling at her new orange dress. He was tempted not to take her to the panorama. But people found his wife pretty. She was a useful flourish for an otherwise serious and ambitious man. Jean-Pierre shrugged and turned back to his notes.

He didn't see Sophie's wide eyes narrow into slits.

"The Channel crossing was dangerous under any conditions," Jean-Pierre continued. For lack of wind he and the American, Dr. Jeffries, had dropped so low they had to jettison their scientific equipment and several bottles of wine, but their balloon had lifted only slightly before swaying near the water again. Jean-Pierre shuddered, remembering. Boot by boot they had begun to strip until hats, belts, breeches, and waistcoats were over the side. Finally they had nothing left to throw. Desperate, they had lightened the basket further by pissing aft. On occasion a few grams could make all the difference, but not this time. Fortunately, a little breeze picked up from the northwest, and nearly as naked as the trumpet-blowing angels that decorated the basket, he and Jeffries had landed in an oak tree in the Guînes Forest.

Suddenly it occurred to Jean-Pierre that he would not have had to share the glory of his Channel crossing if his wife had been aboard and not that American doctor. For the first time he looked with favor on Sophie's light body.

It wouldn't take up much room in a balloon basket.

He put down his pen and reached for it.

One evening a few minutes after Sophie and Jean-Pierre entered the building on boulevard Montmartre that housed the panorama, the gas lamps were lighted and all of Paris came into view.

The audience was seated in the center of a circular painting seventy feet wide and forty-five feet high. Along with the others, Sophie and Jean-Pierre quickly lost all judgment regarding space and distance. The different parts of the picture were drawn to such an exact scale that the result was a perfect illusion. It had been conceived from a perspective of considerable height, and Sophie felt as if she were standing on the roof of the Tuileries—or in a balloon on the rise. Below her, chestnut trees along the boulevards bloomed in rivers of foam, and roses in the Jardins des Bagatelles made an iridescent sea.

Afraid of altitude real or contrived, Jean-Pierre was already scrambling down from the raised seats and so he didn't see Sophie's face glowing in the gaslight, but others were struck by her incandescent smile.

"Hurry up!" said Jean-Pierre. "I feel sick!"

Sophie took her husband's hand as they left the room, but she stared back at the panorama.

The clouds in the round, painted heavens seemed near enough to touch.

Jean-Pierre wasn't alone in his discomfort as he bent his head to his knees. Apart from Sophie, everyone was uneasy, for after all, they could see above the rooftops of Paris from Notre Dame to the Bois de Boulogne, and who but a bird could do a thing like that?

Sophie smiled as if joy was her natural state.

Unknown to Jean-Pierre, during the last few months he and Sophie had worked their way through various forms of dried plant life. There had been a bad moment or two. When she stirred a little yohimbe into his wine, Jean-Pierre told her he was on his way to heaven in a diamond-studded balloon; and after they shared a concoction made from the bark of muira puama, that night he had complained of acute intestinal discomfort during the morning's flight, at about the same time she had to hurry home from the market.

Now there was nothing else to drink or chew.

"So be it!" Sophie wrote in her diary that night.

Then looked up at Jean-Pierre.

"Few women have ascended in balloons," she said, "and none has accompanied a husband so deserving of renown as you. I think the novelty of my presence in the basket would draw attention to yours, don't you?"

Jean-Pierre beamed. His wife had read his mind!

~~11~~

"*INOUÏ!*"

TWO WEEKS LATER Sophie and Jean-Pierre were in Marseille.

"The only place large enough to launch a balloon is on a square surrounded by towers and battlements," he announced. "Just one puff of wind from the wrong direction and we're impaled!

"See?" Snow blew in as Jean-Pierre opened a door of the Abbaye St. Victoire and pointed to Marseille's jagged skyline of spires and crenellated turrets. "The bishop wants us to float just above the Candlemas procession—a disaster!"

He was right. It was still snowing the next morning when the airship rose quickly, then swung against the chimney of a house. As Jean-Pierre jumped onto the slippery roof, the bright green balloon, pierced and losing hydrogen, slowly lowered over the procession. The celebrants screamed and scattered. They dropped their green candles and green loaves of boat-shaped bread in the snow. Moments later the balloon became wedged between the buildings on the narrow street. But finally enough hydrogen escaped to allow the balloon to slide past the windows of the houses and frighten the non-celebrants who were looking out.

When the basket came to rest on the cobbles, a number of Marseille's feral cats came up and rubbed against it. They flexed their claws on the wicker and gazed through the weave at Sophie inside.

Her maiden flight above Marseille had lasted only a few minutes, but that night in her diary Sophie wrote the single word *Inouï!* And it *was* "amazing" that a silk sphere coated with varnish could fly!

Aloft, Sophie's awkwardness fell away.

When they took off from Grasse a month later, her gestures were like a dancer's as she stood on her tiptoes and raised an arm to close an overhead valve, then turned to gauge her speed and lean down to tighten a knot on the netting.

But at first she was disconcerted. Even though she and Jean-Pierre were speeding across the sky, her bonnet ribbons hung straight and not a hair on his head moved. "There isn't the slightest breeze!"

"We are floating in it."

On the clothesline in La Salière, her dresses had danced in a high wind, and had hung hand-in-hand like cutout dolls when it subsided. Even the lightest breeze had rippled the salt grass before moving on. But in the air, except for the sun clocking the hours around the sky, little marked the difference between past and present. Nearby clouds flew in the same current, and so they appeared not to move.

In the air, time seemed suspended; made of stillness and light.

"The sensation is incomparable," Sophie wrote. "It can't be described. It's as if I've come back from another world." She paused for a moment, remembering how Jean-Pierre had gripped the basket and kept his eyes on land. Fear is not a good companion on voyages to enchantment, she thought, then in a sure hand wrote, "I want to be alone in the basket the next time I leave land."

Within a few years Sophie would achieve the celebrity that forever escaped Jean-Pierre. Each time she ascended more people flocked to see her, until one day the crowds in Paris would number half a million.

But fame meant little to someone drawn to wonder.

That same day in a church in Dijon, André Giroux studied the girl in the rolling chair. Her leg had been wounded by rifle fire and she looked up at him beseechingly.

"I'm sorry, mademoiselle," he said. "I've tried my best. Given time, your leg will heal."

"But why is this cure so difficult, monsieur?" asked an onlooker.

She was beautiful, André thought. She reminded him of Sophie. And yet there was a difference. He loved Sophie but he only desired the girl. "I would have to be at least five years older before I could heal someone like her," he said.

André didn't add that love gave, while desire took, and that he must lose such feelings. He must become opaque, like a mirror, so the sick could see their well selves reflected.

As André turned next to a small girl, an old woman began to make her way back down the aisle. He had placed his hands on her, also seemingly without effect. But suddenly the old woman gathered speed, and when she neared the open doorway her laughter echoed in the church as she flung away her cane.

In an inn that evening André watched a spring snow begin to fall as a young servant brought in a newspaper and built up the fire. Then the boy poured a few drops of cassis in a glass of white burgundy and handed it to him smiling. "Takes the chill off a cold night." Tasting his first kir, André deliberated over the menu. He had eaten too many mussels to want anything with a shell; still, he had never had snails. After giving his order, he picked up the newspaper, and in an instant the day's small pleasures—the moment's desire for a beautiful girl, the old woman's laughter, the March snowstorm, the warmth of kir, and the anticipation of escargots— all were overshadowed by the news that Madame Sophie Blanchard was to be the first woman to ascend alone. The event was to take place in a month's time, on April tenth at Sancerre's Goat Cheese Festival.

In Paris a week later, Sophie was surprised when Jean-Pierre arrived from Dieppe, though she should have known that any Frenchman in a waistcoat would want to be at home carving his roast on a cold March Sunday. She had invited

Marc-Emmanuel to dinner, and her mother was coming for a visit.

A few minutes after Marc-Emmanuel walked up the stairs, Isabelle entered the salon. Taking a gray-striped kitten from her cloak, she told Sophie, "Like its mother and grandmother, it prefers to eat at night and sleep under the bed." Isabelle smiled, looking around her. A tray was piled with shining red apples and the tablecloth was immaculate, but the rest of the salon was in slight disarray; her daughter had always been slow to impose order.

Sophie held the kitten in her arms and thought of the superstition about stepping on a cat's right front paw. Once or twice she had wondered what might have happened if her marriage had been postponed, but then she had decided it did no good to dream. Instead, as she did with the bright coins she took from her pocket, from time to time she drew out memories of her childhood with André.

At dinner there was the bustle of new friends. Jean-Pierre shaved thin slices from the leg of lamb Sophie had bought from a passing cart and talked of her solo flight the following month. "I have urged her to do it. People will pay dearly to see a woman alone in the air for the first time!"

Smiling at Sophie, Marc-Emmanuel brought a hamper filled with desserts to the table, then took out a letter from Beaune. She didn't pay attention as he began to read. She knew that during the revolution, when his parents were killed in the Duroc château, he had flattened himself among the grapevines in their vineyard for two days and two nights; since then, letters from Beaune had come from the Durocs' housekeeper, about the weather and making foie gras. So at first Sophie didn't listen to Marc-Emmanuel reading the part about Berthe's sprained ankle.

"My husband had to eat dried sausages for a month, until finally he loaded me on a cart and drove to a church in Dijon," Berthe wrote. "You know the one, Marc-Emmanuel, the plain one, Cathedral St. Bénigne, so dark inside one can scarcely see. But nearly at young André Giroux's first touch I put foot to floor and got on with it. I even threw away my cane!"

Sophie looked up at the sound of his name. She had been staring into the fire, remembering a late winter afternoon like this, years ago, when she and André were twelve or so and still raking salt together. They had come inside and were sitting next to each other on the hearth, toasting baguettes. He had laughed and tried to push hers off her stick and into the coals. But she was tired and sleepy, and so he had toasted her bread for her and spread it with butter. They had smiled at each other, in a way they hadn't before; she wanted to touch his cheek glowing in the firelight. André had gazed at her thoughtfully, as if he knew, and had put his arm around her so she could fall asleep against his shoulder.

"Truly, that boy is a marvel! And such broad shoulders!" Marc-Emmanuel read. He was pleased at bringing Sophie news of her old friend, but when he glanced up at her, he was surprised. Though come to think of it, he had seen that look on her face before, and on André's too. A sudden brightness at hearing the other's name, just as suddenly snuffed out.

Only when Isabelle shifted restlessly in her chair—a movement Marc-Emmanuel took to be uncharacteristic—did he finally understand, and look in alarm at Blanchard.

Jean-Pierre was frowning at the paw prints the kitten was making in the dust. He wanted to scold his wife for her sloppy housekeeping, but he was afraid of offending Isabelle. Besides, Sophie's roast had been delicious, as had the tiny peas.

Marc-Emmanuel unpacked the basket Berthe had sent from Beaune, with its fresh-baked almond cakes, goat cheeses from the Durocs' creamery, and jars of mirabelles. Sophie's eyes glittered at the array but Isabelle only nodded. It's her stillness that gives her the air of mystery, thought Marc-Emmanuel, intrigued.

On April tenth, Sophie was alone in a balloon for the first time.

The instant the ground fell away she felt light, as if she had left her body on the earth. She waved to the innkeeper and his wife in their doorway, and seeing two children working in a field, she tossed them a handful of coins. At the side of the road she noticed a man on horseback looking through a telescope that glinted in the sun.

When he pushed back his hair so he could see, Sophie knew it was André.

Her smile is enchanted, he thought.

She is like a painting, a miniature of a woman drawn in a circle of clouds.

It was as if he held her face in his hands.

She seemed so near.

Though her smile confused him. Sophie hadn't been brave as a child. She had run back and forth along the beach like a shorebird, keeping well away from breaking waves. When he had called to her to come and swim in the sea, she had run off awkwardly down the beach, her arms flung back and flapping like small wings.

Now, seeing her fly through the sky, André thought perhaps Sophie hadn't been meant to walk on the earth.

His mare grew restless with the wait and pawed the ground. The spyglass shook. André swept the sky again and again but Sophie had flown out of sight. Galloping north over the hills when she had gone, finally he reined in his horse and rode back slowly the way he had come.

It wasn't he with the right to ride to Sophie; it was someone else.

One last time André searched the sky, then collapsed the telescope. When Sophie had married, he had wished her gone; had thought her gone.

Now he must wish her so again.

Sophie was caught in a fast updraft, and within minutes she could see the farms and villages beyond Sancerre. In the distance, streams threaded down from the hills and footpaths led to faraway pastures.

The present was much more expansive than she had supposed.

In Paris it had seemed to encompass only a street or a

square, for as soon as someone turned a corner, he was part of then; he was part of what had happened a moment or a day ago. But as the landscape unrolled beneath her and André was lost in its intricacies of light and color, Sophie knew he was no longer a figure in the past.

He was only out of sight, on horseback somewhere beyond Sancerre.

In Paris the next morning, Louis Constant kept the water steaming as the first consul splashed in his tub. Constant was well named for a valet. He had already brushed Bonaparte's favorite green jacket and gotten out a spotless white waistcoat.

Napoleon shouted to his secretary, Méneval, to read him the news.

This wasn't young Baron de Méneval's favorite part of the day, but he preferred it to the times when he was trying to get some work done—writing letters and organizing his notes—and the first consul climbed onto his lap. Maybe he was too sensitive about being pretty-boy handsome, but he didn't like anybody playing with his hair! Besides, he couldn't understand it. Though the military school in Brienne was famous for its homosexual "nymphs," Bonaparte hadn't been among them.

But Méneval read aloud with a will. The position as secretary to the first consul of France was a considerable leap up the ladder.

Along with the rest of Paris that morning, Napoleon paid close attention to the account of Madame Blanchard's first solo flight. Ascensions were costly affairs and therefore infrequent;

PEASANTS WERE OFTEN FRIGHTENED BY BALLOONS AND THEIR PILOTS.

by a woman alone, inconceivable. "Aeronauts are much admired in the cities, and often compared to Christopher
Columbus," the newspaper reported. "But out in the coun-
tryside they are considered supernatural creatures. Peasants
were ready with bats and pistols when Madame Blanchard
landed in a village fifteen miles from Sancerre. Until the police intervened, three men were threatening to kill her."

When Méneval finished reading the article, the first consul
got out of the tub. "Courage is the quality I most admire. It's
unheard of in a woman," Napoleon said thoughtfully as his
valet dried him with a hot towel he had warmed on the stove.

⌒

THE MANY USES OF SILK

A WEEK LATER AT MALMAISON, the château he had helped Joséphine buy in Rueil, northwest of Paris, Napoleon wandered among the faded flowers, kicking at dried stalks of delphinium and hollyhock.

Ordinarily even a dying garden gave him pleasure.

But today Napoleon was preoccupied with the thought that his obnoxious remarks to one mistress or another tended to break them of the spell of being bedded by the first consul of France. The problem was, his actor friend Talma had trained him to woo, not to seduce. He had learned to write love letters where objectionable words could be pruned and the well-turned phrase left to flower.

Napoleon was convinced that after Joséphine's betrayal he would never love again, and he knew seduction required a different strategy. In bed there was no time to write a note when things were going badly. He must develop other tactics.

He called for a carriage and then, in his old gray coat with Méneval at his side, he strolled incognito (or so he liked to think) through the Paris streets. "Well, madame, is there anything new today? And what do people say of that buffoon Bonaparte?" he asked as he made the round of the shops. The first consul enjoyed pretending he was a ham-handed, simple fellow. He was the one who carried the mustard crock to 6, place de la Madeleine, to be refilled; and where after examining the casks of twenty-four varieties, he always pointed to the same one.

But he never went into Odiot's next door. His sister Pauline had bared a breast there for a mold to be cast and a punch cup made, and now Joséphine wanted one too. Napoleon was offended by the very idea—his wife's silver breast sitting on a tray for anyone to see! Instead it was over to the Palais Royal for hats. Napoleon had a standing order at Poupard's for the black bicorne—two points, not three—worn parallel to his shoulders. He was apt to lose his in battle and so he always traveled with a dozen or so, which his valet, Constant, maintained with care.

Napoleon shook his head when he saw the silk shop a few doors down. Joséphine *knew* he was trying to encourage the revival of domestic luxury goods, but still she insisted on wearing imported muslin! All she had to do was put on silk a few times and the weavers would be busy for months. Why, as soon as she stuck an ostrich feather in her hair, the shops were sold out the next day!

"It must be lighter than air," Sophie was saying as she and the silk maker stood in the doorway of 5, place des Victoires.

After an argument with Cusset, Jean-Pierre had begun working with Prelle, whose hand-loomed fabrics were bought by the fanciest women in Paris.

"Lightness is all," Sophie said, holding up a length of pale silk and looking through it for clouds.

Napoleon stopped and gazed at the fabric. He had a passion for silk. He began to hum a little tune off-key, for he had solved his seduction problem. After a particularly boorish remark, to make amends he would slip a silk chemise from beneath his pillow!

"Madame Blanchard—" Méneval said, and Napoleon gave a start.

Why, the courageous aeronaute looks so young and innocent! he thought. He smiled and prepared to make his move.

"—your choice of colors is inspired," said the first consul's handsome secretary. "You seem to be holding a scrap of the sky itself!"

Napoleon glared at Méneval. The fool had taken the words right out of his mouth! He deliberated. Should he mention Madame Blanchard's simple silk gown? White was his favorite color on a woman, it emphasized her innocence. (There was more artifice to Sophie's dress than Napoleon knew, for he could have folded her confection of tiny pleats and stitches into the palm of one hand.)

He was just opening his mouth to speak but that upstart was ahead of him again, talking about women who wore purple on city streets!

"White is so much more appealing on a woman," continued the twenty-seven-year-old baron as Madame Blanchard smiled at him. "Everyone knows it emphasizes her innocence."

Napoleon contained his fury only because even he knew it was no way to seduce. Which was what he wanted to do. He wanted to touch Madame Blanchard's ruched brave shoulder. He wanted to crush her to him and feel the warmth of her skin.

One of the reasons he loved silk was because it covered everything yet hid nothing.

"Madame Blanchard." Napoleon stopped because he couldn't think of anything more to say.

Sophie sank into a curtsey.

On the way home, Napoleon felt a weight in his heart that was nearly pain. But in spite of his desire for the radiant Madame Blanchard, he attributed his unease to one of the attacks that came on occasion, when he was tired and under strain.

13

IN THE VENDÉE

THESE DAYS, WHEN HE SAW SOLDIERS marching off to war, André wished he could join them, for surely in the midst of battle it was impossible to think.

While on horseback he had all the time in the world.

He thought of when Sophie was young and had climbed him like a tree. She had sat on his lap with her knees drawn up to her chin and told him about the tracks of birds in the year's first snowfall. She had wanted to know what he had done that day. No detail was too slight, and the smallest problems had seemed to please her the most. Whether he should heat the hasp over a fire in order to bend it, or pound it into a curve instead.

Sophie had laughed uproariously at his jokes, rocking back until he grabbed her and set her upright again, straight as a washboard, with her eyes on him. It was as close as he had come to anyone. After his father had been killed in the revolution, his mother hadn't been the same.

But he had needed only this small, dark shining thing.

He would go and see Miche, André decided. He would try to get Miche to send him to the front, and if that didn't work, he would get in touch with Duroc.

A week later, André and a priest were standing in a field in the Vendée. It was a mass grave of five hundred republican soldiers, half under the age of twenty-one.

"Young Darruder was no more than a child when he picked up his father's weapon on the battlefield and charged the enemy," the priest was saying. "The boy was killed but people are still suffering all over the Vendée."

"All right," André said. "Let them come."

He turned to the corporal standing nearby. "I will see them in order of age, the youngest first. People are most comfortable in a church, but even a tent would do. No one is to stand in front of me or to the side.

"If water is available I should like a pitcher always at hand."

The old corporal nodded, on orders from Colonel Duroc to look after the young healer. Though the boy didn't seem to need any help. But as he walked toward the village to find a church, the corporal puzzled over the fact that Giroux had asked to be sent to the front. He couldn't figure out why a healer would want to place himself in harm's way. Of course Colonel Duroc had said no, and this had been the compromise.

The fighting was over in the Vendée, but the place was a gaping wound that wouldn't heal.

Several days later the reporter Alain Damagnez took notes. He counted the people in the little church in Guérinière, he counted the people Giroux had healed, and then he wrote this article for *Le Moniteur de Saintonge*.

"Hope has come to the Vendée! The healer André Giroux receives—or works, so to speak—five days a week. More than twenty people file in front of me as I stand by the church door, and they come from everywhere in the province, from Chantonnay to Luçon.

"Numbers are given out and twenty-two people—most of them boys who had been in the fighting—are presented to Giroux. There is a certain M.C. from Fontenay-le-Comte, an eighteen-year-old with a bullet still in his thigh who limps painfully and ten minutes later experiences little difficulty walking. Then a deaf fellow is introduced and when Giroux asks gently what is wrong, he, very surprised, answers, 'I am cured.'

"It is now five-thirty and the twenty-two numbers are finished. There you have it. This is what I saw on Wednesday.

"Were there really cures? Some say yes and others no. For me who saw them, I don't hesitate to answer affirmatively and say it's better to support this man than to denigrate him. What I know is that he makes miracles, as has been said in another article.

"Let us take note that Giroux prescribes nothing, orders

nothing, and counsels nothing. He looks, touches—and one is cured!"

Afterward in the vestry, André poured water in a bowl and splashed it on his face. Running his hands through his wet black hair, he grinned in delight at the nice old corporal.

14

HOW TO CROWN
AN EMPEROR

WELL PAST MIDNIGHT, Napoleon lighted a candle and sat on the floor. Among his hundreds of dolls he picked up the figure wearing a crown and an ermine-trimmed cloak.

No one had known how to organize the coronation ceremony until Napoleon had consulted an old Roman text—now, they'd had emperors! Then the court painter Jean-Baptiste Isabey had ransacked the Paris shops for small dolls and figures and clothed them in papal robes, imperial gowns, and the like. Staging the entrance and seating of the participants was crucial to the success of Napoleon's new empire, for among other things it would establish the pope's rank with regard to his.

Napoleon chuckled as he marched the little papal figure down the aisle behind the emperor. Then he took all of his dolls out of Isabey's model of the Cathedral of Notre Dame.

Surely there was an even better arrangement!

.   .   .

But at breakfast Napoleon's bathrobe drooped untidily around his ankles as he considered his rebellious family. It was absurd, his brothers insisting on wearing ermine when everybody knew it was to be worn only by royalty! And how dared his sisters refuse to carry Joséphine's eighty-pound train, when they knew she couldn't make it down that long aisle alone! With his last shred of detachment Napoleon reflected on the fact that these two details had ground preparations for the coronation to a halt for a solid week.

Suddenly, he screamed.

Napoleon couldn't abide an open door.

Even one only slightly ajar filled him with horror. He shouted until someone shut it, then he helped himself to a piece of chicken.

That ninny of a breakfast servant had to go!

A few days later on the morning of the coronation there was fog along with snow. But the houses and shops were more festive for it. Brightly lighted and decorated with tapestries, blue, white, and red bunting, and fresh-cut greens, everything glowed in the falling snow.

Security was tight. Hussars in white and gold and cavalrymen in red lined the street three deep as figures in lavender robes emerged from the colored haze.

"They're heralds," Jean-Pierre told Sophie. "You can tell by the color."

"What do they do?" Sophie asked.

"They announce things."

"But there are so many!"

Jean-Pierre was counting. "Eighty," he said. "But it only takes one."

Sophie and Jean-Pierre were standing in the Cathedral of Notre Dame with the other invited guests. Napoleon had chosen the bumblebee as his imperial emblem, and thousands had been cast in bronze five inches long to decorate the vast expanse. They could scarcely be seen, but the twenty-four crystal chandeliers, generously faceted and filled with candles, created a magical effect.

"*Vive l'empereur!*" the lavender heralds cried.

Sophie was watching the emperor smile at the yellow-toothed woman standing next to him, when the crowd gasped. The princesses had dropped the empress Joséphine's train and she was frozen in her tracks!

Napoleon walked over to his sisters. "Pick it up or be exiled!" he hissed.

In Rome the next afternoon, strollers in the Villa Borghese gardens watched as an unmanned balloon dropped abruptly, knocked into Nero's tomb and broke off a piece of his crown, then banged on a few rooftops before falling into Lake Bracciano. When the Italian police pulled the basket out of the water they found a pamphlet giving the balloon's origins— Paris—together with the reason for the flight and the date: the coronation of the emperor Napoleon by Pope Pius VII on December 2, 1804.

Word reached Paris the next day.

Sometimes Napoleon's pleasure in his bath occupied him

for two hours, but he stood as soon as he heard the Roman newspapers accuse him of coveting the Italian crown. Flicking lemon-scented bath water on Méneval and Constant, he gesticulated his rage at the aeronaut Louis Garnerin, whose balloon was threatening diplomatic relations in Italy when it should have been honoring the emperor in France.

Watching the breakaway sphere bowl south, Jean-Pierre had considered why he had not been chosen to launch one. Back in 1784 when he was about to make his first ascension from the Champ-de-Mars, a boy from the nearby military school had waved a sword and gotten into Jean-Pierre's balloon. They had struggled and finally the schoolboy soldier— he couldn't have been more than fifteen—had run off.

People liked to say the lad was Napoleon and that his behavior had reflected two key aspects of his character: violence and a desire to rise.

Jean-Pierre suspected a third, a penchant for revenge.

"To the balloonist looking down, the greatest legislator is only the king of bees," he bragged that night to a friend. He neglected to add that these days he was happier looking up. His wife had taken to the sky like a bird and was beginning to wing in a few sous. Why, even with the money he shipped off once a month to the Armants in La Salière, he and Sophie were sure to prosper!

15

CLOUDS

IN LA ROCHELLE, not far from where she grew up, Sophie clipped a little flag to her rigging, then she pulled on a line and smiled when the pennant snapped in the wind.

It would be a fast flight.

Sophie waved to her mother, and turned to the man running up to her airship.

"Perhaps you will help me chart the sky!" said the scientist Jean-Baptiste, Chevalier de Lamarck, waving his ticket of admission. There was no time to mention his disappointing conversation with her husband the year before. Blanchard had complained that balloons obeyed only the wind, and that the goal in the air should be control, not height. It was why Lamarck had been startled to read the aeronaut's wife had attained an unprecedented twelve thousand feet! He determined to meet her when he learned that on another occasion she had left Milan in a violent squall and two hours later was a hundred and twenty miles away in sight of Gênes!

But seeing her this morning, at first Lamarck had hesitated. Young Madame Blanchard looked more like an airborne sprite than a nascent woman of science. Then he shrugged. He had no one else to turn to. His colleagues at the Museum of Natural History refused to support his studies of clouds, which was why he was heading up the Department of Insects and Worms.

"Look at the clouds!" he shouted as Madame Blanchard wheeled up on an east wind. He was a scientist and he *knew* sound rose but he didn't believe it. "You can contribute more to science in one day than Lyonnet has in twenty studying the willow-caterpillar!"

Sound doesn't come down as easily as it goes up, but Lamarck heard Madame Blanchard's laughter as she disappeared behind a cloud. "Lyonnet should have chosen the silkworm—*much* more lucrative!" he heard her say.

"Remember the clouds!" Lamarck shouted, as he wondered why a pretty young girl wanted to fly alone to the edge of the sky.

Piloting her airship on a rising wind, Sophie smiled as she burst through a cloudbank and felt the new layer of cold that signaled greater altitude. She was thinking that in the last year or two she and Jean-Pierre had fallen into a pleasant routine. Each time she flew she searched for a stiff wind to push her high into the heavens, and each time she returned she found her husband more content, because the less he flew the happier he became. As she got out her notebook, she wondered why the Chevalier de Lamarck didn't want to fly through the sky himself.

Sophie was ranging around the sides of clouds and driving up fast currents when suddenly a silent storm ambushed the sky. All around her the clouds changed color and form so quickly they seemed alive; they gathered weight and plummeted, then rose and thinned to the sheen of silk. All around her glowed colors she had never seen before, claret with smoke along the edges, and peach infused with chartreuse. Then lines of light shot through the sky until it was filled with silver streaks. Turning in her basket, Sophie followed the course of light that tore across the heavens. The storm lasted an hour, long enough for her to consider an astonishing possibility: that the dazzling lines weren't lightning as she had first assumed, but cracks and fissures in the firmament where white light spilled through from a vast space beyond the breaking blue shell of sky.

At twilight, when a carriage delivered Sophie to La Salière, Isabelle gazed at her daughter's face. As a child she had been merry as well as solemn, but not after she had married. Now even in the dusk Sophie's face looked sunlit. Another mother might have asked and another daughter spoken, but Sophie and Isabelle walked to the beach, and sitting together in a hollowed-out stone, they listened to the sea.

That night in her old room, for a moment Sophie didn't recognize her face in the mirror, shining like silver.

Two days later Sophie was staring up at the imposing stone building, symmetrical but for the white dome that capped a tower.

Lamarck had invited her to visit the Paris Observatory.

Following him up the long flights of stairs, Sophie noticed that when Lamarck greeted the people coming down, they only smiled or looked away. At the top, in a large bare room framed on all sides with windows, men were grouped around telescopes. They waved to Lamarck but as he walked past, Sophie saw some of them roll their eyes.

It took time for Lamarck to adjust one of the telescopes. He squinted, then tried again. But finally he stepped aside and invited her to look.

"I see a blur of white," said Sophie.

He swung the telescope to a different direction and a greater height.

"I can see over a cloud but not through it."

"That's why the science of the sky needs people like you," said Lamarck. "Telescopes don't work when it comes to clouds. A fellow in England polishes the mirrors in his telescope for sixteen hours straight—his sister spoons him soup so he doesn't have to stop! The buffing helps keep the image from blurring and it's fine for looking at stars, but a shined-up a mirror won't get us through the clouds.

"Please tell me what you saw when you ascended above Passy."

Sophie pulled a piece of paper from her muff. "That day there was a storm and the clouds turned many strange and beautiful colors. I described them the best I could."

Lamarck smiled. "You are observant. Next you must study the celestial architecture of the sky. The shapes of clouds at different altitudes." He handed her a package. "Here is a thermometer. Each time the temperature drops half a degree, it means you've traveled higher up in the sky. You might make note of the kinds of clouds you see." He drew five shapes and wrote words next to them. "Quite likely they will look like one of these."

"You do not fly yourself, monsieur?"

"I have seven children. I do not consider them an obstacle to flight but an opportunity to stay on the ground. And you?" Lamarck was interested in all aspects of science, among them psychology.

"If I had children, like you I would not fly," said Sophie. "The compensation for not having them is that I can."

Later, after he had put her in a carriage, Lamarck was thoughtful as he walked home. Madame Blanchard had not once mentioned her husband.

∽

16

DELIRIUM

"WHAT DO YOU MEAN André is at the front?" said Marc-Emmanuel.

"I was with him behind the lines for a fortnight, following Davout," the old corporal repeated. "Yes, I *know* he's not allowed to go! But he's a man, isn't he? It's *his life,* after all! Besides, he's safe now; they've brought him from Auerstadt to Berlin. He says he knows it was imprudent, and won't do it again.

"When he's well he's going to live in my farmhouse in Boulogne."

André had come down with a fever during the battle of Auerstadt and the old corporal had put him in a surgeon's tent. Time had seemed to come and go, but André had known it was he who had drifted between memory and dream, where bodies were piled on bodies, caked with blood and covered with flies. He had heard his mother call "André," and at the height of his fever, he had thought he was lying on a hot black rock in the summer sun.

But always the memory had returned of the night there was no moon.

He had been fifteen and walking home as Sophie came up the path from the beach, her body a thin black shadow. They couldn't see and so they had felt in the darkness for where the other was.

Suddenly the days and months of wanting Sophie had overwhelmed André.

He had pulled her to him and kissed her many times. But the last had been in a kind of farewell. André had been convinced it would take years of experience in healing before he could both love Sophie and be able to cure.

In his hospital bed in Berlin, when his fever subsided, André wondered if he had been wrong.

In Holland, eight miles from The Hague, Jean-Pierre's good ear caught the sound of wind, then lost it a minute later. It was the only way he knew he was spiraling down, for he was in mist. After pushing the levers in a vain effort to agitate the wings against his downward fall, he lost consciousness.

Though he was still alive, Jean-Pierre had suffered a stroke nine thousand feet above Delft.

His balloon descended slowly, for it takes time for hydrogen to flow out. Had it been spring with the water in the canals catching Vermeer's yellow light, he would have fallen into soft reflected clouds. As it was, his balloon landed on solid ice and glided on a canny wind straight down a narrow canal.

The aeronaut had been expected to land in front of a royal gathering at the Château des Bois—or at least in the neighboring beech forest—and so the townsfolk of Delft dispatched a messenger to The Hague where, in the Château des Bois, the king of Holland was pacing up and down the Orange Saloon.

Just because my brother is the emperor of France doesn't give him the right to demand an embargo on British goods when it would be Holland's undoing! King Louis thought. Passing pots of pretty blooming tulips, behind them he heard his wife sob. One more mark against Napoleon for making him marry Joséphine's yellow-toothed daughter! Louis scratched his syphilitic groin and yelled at Hortense, then turned to the fellow from Delft.

Two hours later the royal carriage drew up to a house on Delft's main canal. King Louis strode through the open door and across the black and white tiles to Jean-Pierre Blanchard. It was a sight that, for him, no alabaster breasts would ever approach. The aeronaut looked adorable lying in a cupboard bed with blue-scarfed children crowded around. Dressed in a blue suit with white embroidery, he appeared to have landed smack in the middle of a blue Delft plate! The king carried the aeronaut to the carriage himself, and back in the Orange Saloon, fussing happily with satin sheets, made up his patient's bed.

When Jean-Pierre woke, he raved of a trap he had designed as a boy where rats were killed by a bullet when they stepped on the trigger that lay between them and good Norman cheese. People hadn't understood his genius then, he shouted, slurring his words only slightly; worse, they mocked his accomplishments in the air! Well, Montgolfier's father hadn't even let him fly in *his* balloon. And when Étienne had sent up a rooster, a sheep, and a duck instead, the sheep had given a kick and the rooster had come back lame!

"*I* went up in *my* balloon!" hollered Jean-Pierre.

"Of *course* you did," said King Louis, fluffing up a pillow.

~

CHAPTER 17

SOPHIE TAKES CHARGE

"HERO!" SOPHIE WROTE IN HER DIARY when she learned of Jean-Pierre's ordeal.

At first she had stared in disbelief at the brief notice in *Le Journal de Paris,* for the king of Holland had failed to send her word of his condition. (Napoleon, on hearing the news as Constant was toweling him off, raised more than an eyebrow at the thought of pretty Madame Blanchard near widowhood, and Méneval vowed to look for another job.)

Sophie knew every one of her husband's ascensions had been accompanied by fear. He had told her that, in Frankfort years before, his left ear had been nicked and deafened by a dueling pistol, but he had told her that facing a bullet was nothing.

Nothing like seeing one's self falling from the sky.

Jean-Pierre's plight galvanized Sophie. She hired a wagon large enough to accommodate a bed for him and set out for The Hague. Scarcely knowing where it was and calling out as they went, she and her driver found the way. As usual the bumping, swinging movement of the wagon frightened Sophie, and reminded her of her wedding day when she and Jean-Pierre had driven to Les Petits-Andelys.

He had had such brave dreams, Sophie thought. He had tried to row through the sky. People laughed at him because his eccentricities, like his gold lace cuffs, were too much on display. But she didn't mind them. Nor did she mind—though he had never said—that his duel had been fought over a woman. For who was she to judge where love should go and where it shouldn't? And who could help where it went, or why?

Sophie was well enough acquainted with wind to know that it didn't go where it ought but where it must.

Several days later, when she reached the Château des Bois, Sophie was humored, fed—and deflected from the care of Jean-Pierre by King Louis, who had dressed him up in an apple-green suit with a pink waistcoat and tie. He had draped the Orange Saloon in white sheets. Now, with flaking tissue falling from the palms of his hands (a symptom of secondary-stage syphilis), the king was brushing his patient's hair.

"Place the bed in my wagon, if you please," said Sophie.

But at home, Jean-Pierre was so quickly disheartened by the indignities of a bedpan and rolling chair that Sophie sent for her mother.

When Isabelle arrived, everyone became more himself. Sophie's heart felt more spacious, as if a door had been thrown wide, and Jean-Pierre's dark thoughts brightened under her untroubled gaze. Marc-Emmanuel (who could never stay away) wondered if those eyes ever burned with desire.

But Isabelle sought nothing.

Soon she and Sophie were absorbed in preparing dinner, walking to and fro from washbasin to chopping board, each anticipating the other, as they had for the years of a childhood. With their graceful movements they might be dancing a minuet, Marc-Emmanuel thought, standing in the kitchen doorway.

Gray-striped kittens played under the table as everyone discussed Jean-Jacques Rousseau over *pot-au-feu*. "He was a great philosopher and without him we wouldn't have had a revolution," said Jean-Pierre. "He was all for the rights of the common man."

"He used to be Napoleon's hero too, and look what all that 'liberty, equality, fraternity' has got us—an emperor who wants to conquer all of Europe and millions of dying men!" Marc-Emmanuel said.

"Rousseau was wonderful, though mad," said Isabelle, and they looked at her and wondered how she knew.

"I know what we'll do," Jean-Pierre told Sophie when she handed him the day's letters. He had gambled while on his trips, and the bills, couched at first in language befitting their slightly famous recipient, had begun to arrive in the form of crude threats. "We'll arrange a tour of Saxon towns for you," he said. "That fellow from across the street will look after me, and his wife can cook a bit and bring it over. Meanwhile, accept the invitation to ascend in Avignon so we'll have a little money coming in."

Sophie nodded. She stuffed the bills in a drawer and wrote to Avignon.

Then she set about designing a new airship.

First she dispensed with Jean-Pierre's heavy gondolas, for she had found that wood had little give and often cracked on landing. Then she set aside his eight-foot oars. Sophie had no interest in trying to direct her travel, and rather than man-handle an unwieldy ship she intended to come as close to the wind as possible. Since there was no time to travel back and forth to Cusset in Lyon, she worked with Prelle, whose factory was nearby.

"Ah, *non*, madame. That will not do," Prelle said the first day, looking at her basket. "It's too small. One tap against a tree and, *pouf*, you are out of it."

Sophie paid no attention. Next she modified the size and style of Jean-Pierre's balloons, which were immense. Any silk sphere, geometrically cut, carefully sewn, and painted with varnish was a costly affair. But each of the many lengths of fabric required for one of his had been eighty feet long, and four or five workmen had needed a week to assemble it.

Sophie's design was more modest—and more economical to construct.

Prelle studied her drawing. "That balloon is *much* too small. If all goes well you will fly up the sky like an angel. But think of the ruckus on changing currents. The silk could be ripped to shreds."

But Sophie was banking on lightness.

"Madame would do well to stick to designing dresses," said Prelle, looking at her condescendingly.

"Keep cutting," Sophie told a workman who had stopped to watch.

The lengths of silk were shorter, narrow, and all the same color.

"No pictures on it?" Prelle asked. "No garlands and signs of the zodiac?"

Within a few weeks Sophie had produced a vessel considerably different from Jean-Pierre's.

"No *color*?" said Prelle.

On the morning of Sophie's flight from Avignon, people laughed and talked as they leaned against the railings of the bridges on the Rhône and gathered in the windows of houses. They watched men play boules and vendors sell fresh lemonade while children chased each other and dogs barked and tore in circles.

But everything stopped when Sophie stepped into the elegant little basket she had discovered long ago in Jean-Pierre's barn. The wicker shone like gold and above it the pale sphere was a shimmering sunlit cloud. Without the added weight of pedals and directional feathers, and with a sleek, scaled-down balloon, when the handlers released the lines, her airship flew higher than the rooftops in less than a second.

As sometimes happened in those days, the crowd stared as if transfixed.

Back in 1784 in St. Cloud, thousands had fallen to their

knees at the sight of a balloon overhead, and once when de
Rozier had had a minor accident in the air, the spectators
had raised their arms as if to catch him. Their reactions
were new and moving demonstrations of fellow feeling, for
even the poorest peasants could watch an airship swing
through the sky. Though they might not have been able to
put it into words, better than anyone they knew why ballooning was emblematic of the democratic spirit abroad in
France.

But their connections to Sophie were more personal.
Many people knew she had taken up her stricken husband's
work and it reminded them of the sacrifices they too had
made. As they watched her soar above them through limit-
less skies, they thought of the freedoms they had fought for.
But when they saw coins rain down from her basket, in her
gesture of generosity they forgot for a moment the years of
breadlines and barren fields, and loved her for it.

The next morning, as she sat at Jean-Pierre's writing table,
Sophie didn't know she was becoming a symbol for the people of France. It would be some time before she realized this,
and longer still before she saw that her fame could be put to
use. Now she opened her notebook and studied the observa-
tions she had made in the air the day before.

When she had risen, at each half-a-degree fall in temperature she had drawn a profile of the clouds she had seen, and
when she descended, as a check, she had made sketches at
each half a degree's increase. Now Sophie found that both

times, the same cloud forms had occurred at the same temperatures. Comparing them to the shapes on Lamarck's list,
she wrote a name next to each drawing.

When she finished, she sent her chart to him by courier.

PART TWO

SEPTEMBER 1808–
JULY 1819

NAPOLEON FALLS IN LOVE

SITTING IN THE THEATER in Erfurt, Germany, the emperors of France and Russia and the kings and princes of the rest of Europe were tired. For the two weeks of the Congress of Erfurt they had held meetings and reviewed each other's troops. They had gone hunting, though Napoleon's valet, Louis Constant, was appalled at the cloth partitions—like *holding* pens, he thought!—used to prevent the escape of the sixty stags the nobles had then brought down in an afternoon.

The royals and their wives had danced at balls and been entertained in the little Erfurt theater. Napoleon had even imported his friend Talma for the occasion, and one of the actor's lines in Voltaire's *Oedipus* had caused a stir. "The friendship of a great man is a blessing of the gods," said Talma, whereupon the czar of Russia had grabbed the emperor of France and hugged him. As they stood and held hands to great applause, Napoleon thought he was well on his way to conquering most of the world.

Napoleon Bonaparte, circa 1809

By the last night, everybody had used up their best clothes and eaten too much at state dinners in nearby castles. Loosening the collars of old shirts and unbuttoning the waists of last season's gowns, they began to nap even before the concert began.

As he entered the theater, Napoleon glanced up at the box reserved for foreign visitors, then stared at the delicate face etched in the frieze of drowsing heads.

He turned to Goethe. Napoleon had asked to meet him, for he had read his *Sorrows of Young Werther* seven times, and at breakfast the famous writer had seemed to know everyone.

Napoleon nodded to the foreign visitors' box.

"Who's she?"

"The wife of the aeronaut Blanchard," replied Goethe. "I'm collecting my mother's letters, and she wrote of seeing him in Frankfort in 1785. She called them the happiest days of her life. Of course, I may be adding a nuance or two! Though I seem to recall some sort of duel. I calculate my mother to have been fifty-one at the time and Blanchard all of thirty-three."

Standing next to Goethe was the silk maker he had commissioned to design a curtain for his theater in Weimar. "I once constructed a balloon for Blanchard," said Cusset. "The aeronaut didn't seem to care much for his wife then, after having been married less than a year. Madame Blanchard has become famous in her own right in France, and now she's been invited to ascend in a few Saxon towns."

The emperor wasn't listening.

"She is a woman of great daring," he said. "I've met her before, I just didn't recognize her with the wig."

In fairness to Napoleon, Sophie had never before been the arresting presence she was this evening. Her slight figure seemed to be carved from the ivory of her gown and her features looked even more fragile beneath the white powdered wig.

Napoleon took out his opera glasses.

When the concert began, it sounded to Sophie as if the soprano's voice was filled with memories. The song with its falling notes had a nostalgic quality too. It made her think of summer days in La Salière when she and André had hooked bare feet on the rungs of chairs in any cottage and felt at home. As the next tune rose in a plea, Sophie recognized it immediately, for she had danced to it on her wedding day—until the fiddler had put down his bow. But tonight the woman kept singing, and this time Sophie turned across the square until she reached André. Over and over, slow moving as a cloud, his hands left his hips and touched her face.

When the song ended, Goethe clapped heartily. Years before, Mozart had set one of his poems to music and it seemed to be holding up well. Looking at the foreign visitors' box, he was pleased to see Blanchard's wife smiling.

That evening, each time Napoleon gazed at Sophie his eyes rested on the face of a woman he would never again forget. He wanted to talk to her but the czar was holding his hand.

When the concert was over, Cusset walked to the stairs that led to the balcony. "What a coincidence!" said Sophie, pausing on her way down.

"Be assured, madame," said Cusset. "It is never a coincidence when a man stands before a beautiful woman."

"Then it must be coincidence that brings us to Erfurt."

"Again, logic will out," Cusset said in his kindly way. "Your fame has seated you in this theater, where my work has given me a role to play." Seeing her vivid face, he recalled what he had told her when she was a girl—that silkworms waited some time before their wings were grown and they could fly.

Surely Madame Blanchard was in full flight!

As he handed her into the carriage sent by her hostess, Cusset smiled. "When we meet again, madame, as now, coincidence will not be the cause."

19

LOST ON THE
GROSSER BEERBERG

"MY GRANDFATHER WOULD have loved these seams," a man confided to Sophie two weeks later in Weimar's largest square. It was the last day of her Saxon tour and she was checking Jean-Pierre's old yellow balloon bag, for her small new one could not accommodate enough hydrogen for long flights.

"Grandfather was a tailor, and these seams are probably as long as have ever been sewn!" the man said. "Though perhaps those on the sails of our largest ships are longer. A lot of work goes into this, assembling the pieces and matching the edges. And there is considerable shaping here too, am I right? Curious. An elongated sphere. I wonder why.

"But forgive me," he said, bowing over Sophie's hand. "I am Johann Wolfgang von Goethe. I saw you in Erfurt."

"And I am Sophie Blanchard. The balloon is one designed by my husband years ago, monsieur."

"With good reason, I am sure, Madame Blanchard. But I

dabble a bit in science and I can't help think so tapered a balloon could twist in a strong lateral wind."

"Can you suggest a better shape?"

"Perfectly round, madame."

Sophie looked at Goethe gravely. "Perhaps you can help me. This package arrived today from Paris. It's a barometer—and a thermometer as well, though Monsieur Lamarck has already given me one of those."

"I've heard of him," said Goethe. "He was very ill as a young man and confined to an attic room. For a year he studied clouds through his skylight. But he had the bad luck to give them French names even his colleagues couldn't fathom! And worse luck to publish in the issue of a journal next to an article on predicting weather with astrological data!"

"That's why the other scientists disparage him," said Sophie.

"I follow the work of a different man, myself. Howard in England has given his clouds Latin names every scientist understands. I use his symbols every day in my journal to indicate the weather.

"But let's have a look at what the French have sent," said Goethe. "No doubt they want to know how high an angel can fly!"

Charmed by pretty women, he smiled at Sophie.

"Probably I am a theater director as well as a poet because I was given marionettes and a little stage as a boy. But what in your childhood has led you to this?" he asked with a nod at her balloon. Goethe was sure he knew. The aristocracy was mad about ballooning. It gave them something to do. With her erect carriage and cultivated accent, he wouldn't be surprised if she were the daughter of a duchess.

An hour later, on his way home, Goethe smiled to himself. Young Madame Blanchard couldn't have lived in a peasant village until she was sixteen!

"*Non!*" yelled Napoleon, wet and angry in his bathtub in Paris. "*C'est impossible!* They lie! It can't be!"

It was. Just two weeks after he had seen her in Erfurt, Sophie was lost.

Quickly Méneval finished translating the message from Germany: "The French aeronaute ascended from Weimar and has not been seen since. Mysteriously, her basket has been found but not her yellow balloon."

Méneval looked up. "That *is* mysterious. How could—"

Napoleon grabbed the message and tried to read the German text, then threw it on the floor. He was beside himself.

No protection was to be found on Madame Blanchard.

On her no slick thick layer of fat like that which warmed and padded a goose to ward off the cold!

"Those stupid Germans will never find her!" said Napoleon. They were always rising up and he was always putting them down. It was like dealing with a bunch of pop-up dummies.

Constant stopped pouring hot water and tried to wrap the emperor in a towel.

Méneval picked up the wet shreds of the courier's message and dried them on the stove. Perhaps some good news could be salvaged. But no. Despite the efforts of many German citizens, Madame Blanchard remained unfound after a five-hour search, at which time night had fallen. The rescue effort was to resume first thing the next morning.

Napoleon bellowed for his horse—white, of course.

Claude Méneval seized the initiative. He locked the emperor in the bathroom and wouldn't let him out. The plan for taking Austria required every minute of his time, Méneval said. The young baron longed to ride to Madame Blanchard on that fast horse with the crown and letter *N* branded on one white haunch.

"*I* will go in your stead," said Méneval.

"You will *not*! Send for her mother."

At supper the emperor left his *poulet à la Provençale* untouched.

He didn't notice when an aide eased him out of one chair—whose arm he had begun to dig at with his knife—and into another, which he had already wrecked.

Two days later a second message from Weimar announced Madame Blanchard's rescue and explained the mystery of why the basket had been recovered before she: "As her balloon began to lose hydrogen, in order to lighten the load, Madame put her feet in the rigging, then cut away the basket. Suspended in the cords she flew partway over the Grosser

Beerberg—nine hundred feet high—before she and her slowly collapsing balloon dropped to earth.

"When unkempt trappers on the mountain's north face came upon Madame Blanchard she was covered in yellow balloon silk, and icicles were clinging to the collar of her black cloak."

Napoleon's jaw dropped.

No fat, no blanket, no common sense!

But what courage!

He was still incensed that his secretary had prevented him from galloping to Madame Blanchard's aid, and Constant and Méneval had a bad time of it until they heard Duroc call from the next room.

"Send him in!" yelled the emperor.

And the lady as well?

Why not?

Marc-Emmanuel and Isabelle found the emperor sulking in his towel. But as soon as he was introduced to the mother of Madame Blanchard, Napoleon became gallant, to impress. With a broad smile he gave her the good news of her daughter.

Who at that moment, bandaged arm and foot, was layered in fur robes and tucked into the corner of a small sleigh. Despite her injuries and her lost equipment, Sophie was riding enchanted down a lower slope of the Grosser Beerberg. Oblivious to the tall, dark pines and the chalets shrouded in the season's first snow, she was enchanted because she had flown for the first time through the night sky. Through air the softness of velvet. At dawn the stars hadn't seemed to be stars at all, but light shining through perforations in the firmament.

On her way back to Weimar, Sophie designed a basket in the shape of a cradle so that she could sleep aloft.

ON HEARING THE NEWS

20

AT HOME ON RUE CASSETTE, Sophie had begun reading the newspaper aloud to Jean-Pierre. Some mornings, though neither knew it, she and Méneval chorused the news together. But today Sophie read silently the article announcing the arrival in Paris of the healer André Giroux.

"After more than a half dozen years of travel up and down the Atlantic coast, and long periods of work in the Vendée and a stint at the front, thirty-year-old André Giroux has finally come to Paris. He is not what one might expect of a healer," the paper reported. "He is a strapping fellow with a ready smile. The son of peasants, he carries himself like a nobleman but turns not the poorest soul away."

An hour later, it was nothing to ask the man from across the street to carry Jean-Pierre down the stairs, and nothing to fold and fasten the rolling chair and place it in a carriage. For Sophie was impelled by two thoughts—that André would heal Jean-Pierre, and that at last she would see him.

As Sophie and Jean-Pierre moved slowly in the line of people across the candlelit narthex of St. Julien-le-Pauvre, monks circled the altar, swinging incense. But something sharper and more familiar in the air reminded her of La Salière, and she decided that during the war years the church must have been used to store salt. Disoriented, Sophie bent down to speak in Jean-Pierre's good ear and straighten the blanket on his knees.

When she glanced up, she found they were much nearer than she had thought.

They were quite close to André.

Sophie blushed when she saw his hands. She had clung to memories of him until she thought they had faded. Now she realized that instead, worn with use, they had merged into the present without her knowing. In the bed under the eaves in Les Petits-Andelys and in Paris, André's hand had been on her. For years she had been upending the past into the present as if it were an empty jar. Sophie's knees buckled and she leaned awkwardly on Jean-Pierre's rolling chair. She pushed against the handles in such a way that the chair was propelled forward and only narrowly missed the cane of an infirm.

André's concentration faltered on an ailing boy.

A few minutes later he was placing his hands on Jean-Pierre's left side. But perhaps because the aeronaut could not summon the will or because he himself could not concentrate, Blanchard's condition remained the same. Shifting so that Sophie was outside his field of vision, André focused his attention again on Blanchard. But after following the course of the stroke one last time, along the left side of the face and down the body, he shook his head and turned away.

André could not tell Sophie why he had been unable to heal Jean-Pierre Blanchard. He could not tell her that probably it was because he was unable to wish perfectly for her husband's cure. They parted with scarcely a word exchanged, each stunned at his failing to heal—and at inhabiting a present they could not share.

Later André realized he hadn't even heard her voice, and Sophie, hurt and uncomprehending, was sure he no longer cared.

Two weeks later Jean-Pierre died quietly. Cradling him in her arms, Sophie recalled that as a boy he had filled a bowl with water, and rubbed his hands with soap until a bubble freed itself and floated on the heat of a candle. It had given him his first notion of the possibility of flight. The fragile sphere had shaped his life, and with it, she and Jean-Pierre had made a marriage. Sophie cried, recalling the old orange waistcoat he had worn in the days when they had met and married and come to Paris. She would find it for his funeral, and tuck a length of gold balloon silk around him in the casket.

There was no money for a proper ceremony in Paris. When she opened the drawer and counted up the bills, they amounted to more than sixteen thousand francs, an enormous sum! Instead she would take Jean-Pierre's body to Les Petits-Andelys with its memories of the generous-breasted women he had loved.

A few days later, sitting in the church on the village square and cushioned by his soft sisters, Sophie thought of Jean-Pierre's courage. None of his relatives or his old neighbors in the pews knew he had been frightened each time he flew. And because of this, only she knew how brave he had been.

In Boulogne that day, André held a letter and walked around the farmhouse several times. He went into the barn and came back out. He went down and stared at the Seine.

He could not get used to a world where Sophie was free.

Only after taking in the news of Blanchard's death was André struck by the letter's author. He had known Isabelle Armant all his life. She had made him practice his numbers and letters, and she had taught him not to hitch up his pants when he bowed. But she had never been like the women gossiping at the village well. She had never interfered. It surprised him that she would do so now. Finally he decided that her watchfulness had been there all along, but like a good tile roof, it had gone unnoticed because it protected so well.

He would wait a week before he went to Sophie. No more.

That same afternoon, as soon as Napoleon learned of Blanchard's death, he invited Duroc for supper.

Now he waved a forkful of *poulet à la Provençale* in Marc-Emmanuel's face. "What? Blanchard wasn't rich?"

"Far from it. He was in bad shape."

Marc-Emmanuel was puzzled by his interest in Blanchard. He had mentioned him only because he knew Bonaparte was fond of riches-to-rags stories. They were such a foil for his success—the scholarship boy at the École Militaire who had become the emperor of France.

"And now Madame is poor?" Napoleon asked.

"As a church mouse. She is making arrangements to fly all over, in Italy and the like, to try to pay off her husband's debts. She will have to sell her empire bed, and can scarcely afford to buy coffee."

Marc-Emmanuel was used to seeing naked emotions play across Bonaparte's face, among them greed, anger, and ambition. To say nothing of lust. But here was a more subtle display of sympathy and compassion.

"Perhaps I might be of some help," said Napoleon. Smiling at Duroc, he noticed for the first time that his friend had a bad head cold. He sent for Méneval to build up the fire—he liked a hot room himself—and soon the tent was steaming.

When Bonaparte was dozing in his chair, Marc-Emmanuel turned to Méneval. "Now, what's all this about Madame Blanchard?"

"You know these peasant types," said Baron de Méneval to Vicomte Duroc, masking his jealousy with disdain. "Anything for a conquest."

AFFAIRS OF STATE

ONLY A FEW DAYS LATER NAPOLEON sent for Madame
Blanchard to come to Malmaison. He was prevented from re-
specting a longer period of mourning by a commitment to go
and wage war in Austria.

The affairs of an empire could not wait for grief; at least,
that was what he told himself. Besides, it was nearly tulip
season and Joséphine was off in Holland visiting Hortense.

The day in early March was unseasonably warm. On the
pond his wife's black swans swam in monogamous pairs.
They rose up and snapped their red beaks at Napoleon in his
little boat as he made his way to the pretty columned spot he
had chosen for his rendezvous with Madame Blanchard.

He had already written the widow a letter inviting her to
become his official aeronaute, then added his condolences. "But
you must be very sad, chère madame. To ascend alone in a balloon to great heights is appealing only when one can descend
to a life shared with such a man as Monsieur Blanchard. But to

be alone both in the air and on the earth—this is insupportable. Allow me to ease your cares, a little." And on it went.

Napoleon had arranged for Madame Blanchard to be ferried across the pond in a small craft ten feet long with an open cabin decked out in lace-edged cushions and hung with fine paintings and an embroidered flag of the empire. While he waited, he walked briskly—nearly marched—up and down the little terrace in front of the Temple of Love, for though surprise attacks of enemy solders hadn't the power to unnerve him, a woman could.

As the little boat approached the temple, Madame Blanchard stood. She was sheathed in black taffeta, like his sword in its scabbard, and her skin glinted in the sunlight like polished steel.

But her eyes were soft behind the long black veil.

Napoleon wasn't often drawn to a woman whose face revealed so much.

Which is to say there was an exception.

A friend once noticed that the only place Napoleon was contented other than on a battlefield was in Malmaison's gardens. There he was genial, sensitive, even good, said the friend; capable of showing pity and indulgent of human weakness.

Today Napoleon pulled out every stop.

He had his Egyptian gazelle accompany them on the gravel path around the Temple of Love, and it sneezed charmingly when he fed it snuff (though a nearby parrot shrieked "Bonaparte!" in suspiciously high-pitched tones). As soon as church bells began to ring, Napoleon placed a cautionary hand on Madame Blanchard's arm. He said the bells were his favorites, from the sixteenth-century church next door, and he didn't like the sound of footsteps as they tolled.

In the hothouse Napoleon didn't mention Joséphine's deep interest in flowers, and actually in all the natural sciences; she was importing eucalyptus trees in the hope their flowers would nourish bees and promote the production of honey. Instead, when his guest stopped before a particularly beautiful orchid, he smiled modestly and acted the simple gardener. He talked about how as a schoolboy he had been given a patch of earth and had planted a little garden. How he still enjoyed tilling the soil.

Next he drew Madame Blanchard into the hundred-foot-long art gallery. At first he had been tempted to get Antonio Canova's statue of him out of storage. But he had hesitated, not because it was undraped (after much thought he decided a widow wouldn't be shocked at the sight of his nude stone body), *non,* the problem was, the statue was ten feet tall, and he—the real Napoleon—liked to think he was a bit taller than five feet four inches. In the end, the Canova statue of Mars the Peacemaker, otherwise known as Napoleon, stayed in storage for the same reason it had been put there in the first place; the emperor did not wish to expose himself to ridicule.

Napoleon paused before an unusual erotic sculpture by Houdon, asked Madame Blanchard if he might address her by her first name, then repeated his proposal that she represent the empire as its appointed balloonist complete with annual stipend.

After supper servants positioned four silk cushions on the

lawn and held torches while Napoleon taught Sophie to play prisoner's base. It was his favorite game. What more could he do? he asked himself as he panted around the pillows.

At supper he had fed her caviar with a tiny spoon.

Finally, singing a Spontini aria off-key, he handed her back into the barge.

Napoleon gazed at Sophie's slender arms clasped behind her head. Her long black gloves reminded him she was recently bereaved and when he bent to kiss her cheek, it was a chaste kiss; one he might give his grandmother. Under the circumstances, it was the correct kiss, he thought. But halfway to her other cheek, he lost his resolve and kissed Sophie's mouth. Raising his hand, Napoleon made a twirling motion, and while the boatman poled them about for a moment longer, he kissed her as gently as he was able.

Sophie knew no one except an emperor would approach a grieving widow.

A boy from a peasant village would wait much longer.

But she had no hope that André would come to her.

Later Sophie would cry, remembering Napoleon's kisses. Her heart had beat unevenly, as if it hadn't known what to feel. She had loved Jean-Pierre as best she could, and as much as he had wished. And though she had no reason to hope for André's love, she did. But while she wished in vain for one man, she had enjoyed the attentions of another; then cried.

Seeing Bonaparte the next morning, Marc-Emmanuel was appalled. He hadn't been looking forward to hearing lewd comments about Sophie—as a rule the emperor insisted on imparting every detail of his passionate encounters. And he hadn't wanted to listen to him brag about what had gone on in the boat he knew was nothing more than a tarted-up, floating feather bed.

But anything would have been better than this: Bonaparte was being circumspect; worse, he was dreamy!

And that smile!

How far this had all gone was difficult to tell.

Yet just a day later the emperor seemed under strain—because, Marc-Emmanuel assumed, he had learned of threats of conspiracy at home at the same time that he was preparing for war in Austria. Though possibly playing a role as well was Napoleon's infatuation with Sophie; he was off to war, didn't want to leave her, and so on. But it wasn't clear what direction this might take.

To divorce from Joséphine and marriage to Sophie?

Or to a love nest on the outskirts of Paris?

Marc-Emmanuel resolved to dash Bonaparte's hopes, whatever they might be. If nothing more, he could at least give André Giroux a clear field.

"You say Blanchard was a great deal older?" the forty-year-old emperor asked eagerly. "I thought as much. While Sophie has such a youthful air."

Then Marc-Emmanuel played his trump card. Not only was thirty-one-year-old Madame Blanchard far from being a child, she was unable to bear one.

Napoleon fell into a silence that lasted nearly through supper.

They were eating *poulet à la Provençale* again and drinking the usual indifferent wine. Given the circumstances, Marc-Emmanuel should have known better than to complain about the boring fare. Napoleon reddened. Ordinarily he added water to his glass of Chambertin but now he took it straight. He was about to wage war, was he not? the emperor thundered. He would be away from good French food for weeks, perhaps months! Recently, Napoleon had shouted that a minister he detested was nothing more than common shit in a silk stocking. Now he shouted the insult at Duroc.

Then suddenly the emperor began to shake and roll his eyes.

He fell from his chair in convulsions.

Marc-Emmanuel was horrified but not surprised. He had known since military school that Bonaparte was subject to fits. After he and Méneval had undone the emperor's collar and loosened his white suede breeches, they settled him on one of his camp beds. Then, calling for his horse, Marc-Emmanuel galloped to Boulogne, a mile or two southwest of Paris. A cold rain was falling and the towpath was slick along the Seine. He took to open fields when he could, but it was nine o'clock when he entered the church where a young man stood before André while others waited in line.

As soon as he recovered, Napoleon sent for Sophie.

Then he turned his attention to his bedroom. All the furnishings in each of his palaces, even his books, were arranged in the same way so he could place a hand on them at will. And everything was identical. For example, he always had two beds in his room—small, made of metal, covered with worn blankets, far from seductive.

Taking Méneval's arm, the emperor walked into his wife's rooms. Directing his secretary to scoop up a shawl here, a rug there, he opened an armoire and looked at her gowns— at the transparent muslin and deep décolletage. What did the newspapers call Joséphine's style? Fashionably undressed? Unfashionably nude? It amounted to the same thing!

"You cannot wear this!" Napoleon would shout nearly every night as tinted wigs, pink ones and blue ones, toppled from Joséphine's dressing table; no one ever knew how. Then her imported cotton gowns were on the floor and he was stamping on them. A seamstress could be counted on to prick her finger and the hairdresser Duplan always waved his hands and cried. Maids were fired and were back the next day. Every time, getting ready seemed as if it would never end.

Finally, gown approved, flowers in place, diamonds sparkling, tiaras and jeweled belts secured, tendrils obedient, and slippers polished, Joséphine was a vision. The emperor shook his head, remembering. Preparing a regiment for battle was nothing to dressing his wife for dinner!

He climbed back in bed and gazed out the window at the rain.

At that moment, Sophie was on her way to Cusset's house in Paris. Despite being in mourning she had decided to attend a dinner the silk maker was giving; they worked together often now, and it would disappoint him if she sent her regrets.

When he saw Sophie standing in the doorway, Cusset held up his monocle and nodded his approval. Her narrow dress with its long train was striking. He had ordered it sewn of his thinnest, blackest silk. Smiling and shaking hands, Cusset made his way through the group of people waiting to present themselves to Madame Blanchard. She scarcely had room to breathe! he thought, signaling to Daguerre. They had met a few years before when he had been installing a theater curtain at the Paris Opera and the boy walked by on a tightrope. Daguerre had laughed and said, "I'm apprenticed to the set designer, but the acrobats are teaching me all they know!"

Now the young man stretched his legs in the air and the guests parted, clapped, and laughed. When he was back on his feet, he bowed before Madame Blanchard and introduced himself.

"We have met before, madame."

"Years ago in the Cormeilles hills," said Sophie smiling.

Over supper the scenery painter described his dream of using sunlight to fix an image. "I want to seize the fleeting light and imprison it. I want to fix the moment forever," he said. Gesturing to the damask tablecloth and the bowls of white stephanotis glowing in the candlelight, he added, "Wouldn't it be lovely to preserve this moment?" Sophie smiled at Daguerre. She didn't want to hurt his feelings, but she had learned that the surfaces of things meant little. It was the layers of the past that gave substance to the present, and how was one to capture that?

A bustle of activity surrounded the announcement that the emperor's carriage awaited Madame Blanchard.

Half an hour later, when Méneval had taken Sophie's cloak and delivered her to the emperor's bedroom, tiny drops of rain sparkled in her hair. Seating her on a low stool, Napoleon removed her wet boots. Then he led her to a small bed positioned close to his. He had made it look like a daybed. At one end he had piled ivory cushions, the sides embroidered with the letter *J* turned to the back; at the other end a pug wheezed and snuffled on a white cashmere shawl.

As instructed, a tight-lipped Méneval had already blown out most of the candles; he had even been told to bank the fire! Now he drew the heavy velvet curtains and left the emperor and Madame Blanchard to the intimate disarray of the sickroom.

When Marc-Emmanuel and André walked in, Napoleon was touching Sophie's arm.

She and André stared at each other.

Her cheeks were rosy and her stocking feet were pale against the black train that fell to the floor like a shadow.

André knew little about the subtleties of attraction and flirtation and even less about the moments that contained both, without significance. What he saw was this: a man unbuttoned in bed with his hand on a bootless, happy girl.

He scowled.

Once a wedding veil had separated him from Sophie, and now an empire.

André's hand went to his sword.

With a warning glance Marc-Emmanuel skimmed over the introductions. Bonaparte was capable of stunning cruelty if he scented a rival. "Emperor, you seem remarkably restored."

"*Oui, oui*," Napoleon said jovially. But the attack had taken
its toll. When Marc-Emmanuel suggested that André might
prevent a recurrence during the coming campaign in Austria,
the emperor was quick to agree. Like most Corsicans he was
superstitious. For him, the laying on of hands was only a
step away from witchcraft and therefore appealing.

Despite his recent ordeal, Napoleon was the most relaxed
of the four. He treated Sophie with an ease that ought to
have offended no one but did. Marc-Emmanuel worried that
this newly engaging emperor might win his suit, while André read into it the arrogance of a man about to have his way
with a woman.

Or already had.

Only Sophie was not affronted. She could not forget the
stilted encounter with André in St. Julien-le-Pauvre and she
was hurt that he had not come to see her after Jean-Pierre's
death. Unsure of André's feelings, she decided to try to make
him jealous, and so she smiled when Napoleon smiled at her.
Daringly, she stretched out a little foot to display a pretty
instep.

Marc-Emmanuel found the whole business irksome and
wanted to put an end to it. At the same time he noted that
André's eyes hadn't left Sophie's face.

For a moment the only sound was the hiss of the dying
fire.

Then the emperor clapped his hands.

"So, Giroux, let's get on with it!"

André looked here and there. He rubbed his hand
thoughtfully over the hacked-out arm of a chair and grasped

his sword again. He went to the window and gazed at nothing.

Finally he turned to them.

"I cannot help," he said.

And walked from the room.

"Let him go," Napoleon said gently into the stunned silence. "Let him go, let him go, let him go."

Nearly sang it, off-key. Then looked shyly at Madame Blanchard.

There was no denying the sweetness of his smile.

"Put your boots on, Sophie," Marc-Emmanuel said. "I'm taking you home."

GIFTS

IT WAS STILL RAINING THE NEXT MORNING when André went outside to split logs. His black cape spun around him and the pile of wood grew quickly as he thought of Sophie's flushed cheeks and pale feet.

Her lover's hand on her arm.

The sounds of chopping and swearing went on for hours.

In the weeks that followed, André devoted himself to the sick. Time and again he banished Sophie from his thoughts, only to have her return. But slowly came the grace of cure, the recompense for loss of her.

One morning, looking out his kitchen window, André was surprised to see that his horses had shed their winter fur. Their new coats gleamed in the bright sunlight and the brown Seine was splattered blue.

It was spring.

· · ·

Even Marc-Emmanuel had the sense to stay away the day early in April that Sophie put on a long black veil for the second time and walked with her mother at the head of a little cortege. Together they buried Georges Armant in the cemetery of La Salière. Sophie's eyes were blurred with tears of different sorts. She was sad because she had loved her father, but she was also sad because they had been so unlike, he had often felt a stranger to her.

After the ceremony, the villagers reminisced about the day Isabelle had first come to La Salière. Old Georges had been old even then, and he had never been well. But he was handsome—*had* been—and tall for a Frenchman. You might say they took each other in, Georges and Isabelle. He had given her a home and she had raked the salt when he couldn't. The baby—Sophie—had come early, as best anyone could tell. Though she might have come on time. But one thing was certain. No one had lived lighter on the earth than had old Georges Armant. He had never an unkind word to say nor a kind one either, and the women who gossiped at the well said such a man was easy to forget.

And so, as soon as they had him in the ground, everyone crowded around Sophie. They had heard the stories—that she flew all over France without a map and found out where she was by calling to people below; that when she could, she gave away her earnings from a flight, and always tossed coins from her basket.

The peasants knew exploring the skies was a perilous undertaking. After all, there Sophie was, thousands of feet above the earth, alone in an open basket and only inches away from highly flammable gas. They heard that in Naples she had risen so high the sky looked black, and that two miles above Milan the sun had been so bright she couldn't see! The dangers were no fewer on the ground, for she'd been lost somewhere in Germany and nearly been snagged by a windmill in Butte-aux-Cailles. And she was always being pulled out of rivers and lakes. Why, it was a mercy she hadn't landed in the Atlantic! Now, peering at her and plucking at her sleeve, the good people of La Salière asked why anyone would want to fly.

Over the years, Sophie had met most of the world's first airmen. Some were aeronauts with the souls of merchants, who wanted to travel from Paris to Toulouse with a load of mirrors and bring back poultry and eau-de-vie. She knew that scientists were trying to accommodate them, for she had seen their drawings of tall aerostations designed to indicate the wind direction at different heights. To fly to Toulouse with those mirrors, the scientists claimed, a businessman would have only to rise to the appropriate airstream and enter the flow! But not all aeronauts were entrepreneurial. After all, Jean-Pierre and Pilâtre de Rozier had competed for glory in the air, while Étienne Montgolfier had been interested in the science of flight.

Sophie's reason was different, and simpler. She flew for the moment when she separated from the earth. For the moment when a tie—of which she had been unaware—came undone. On every flight she looked for a storm to push her through a fissure in the heavens, and she liked to help the scientists fit a piece or two into the puzzle of the sky. But what compelled her into the air was the moment when clouds flew with her on a wind she couldn't feel. For Sophie, flight was freedom, a gift that was rooted in surprise: the instant she let the wind take her, her life, strictly determined on the earth, became in the air a trackless arabesque.

But Sophie had not been raised to talk of such things. Instead she said that flying was like floating on water.

Which was also true.

In the Armants' cottage, while Isabelle readied the table with cakes, Sophie held the hand of the frail old fiddler. She wanted to thank him for playing a song years ago to try to set her free, and tell him that now she was. But then another villager came up and the knot of mourners loosened. When Sophie looked for the fiddler he was gone.

～

VIENNA

IN PARIS, as soon as Marc-Emmanuel walked into her salon, Sophie handed him a letter that had arrived while she
was away.

He read it quickly, then turned to her.

"Do you see?" he said. "Do you see what comes of flirting
with the emperor of France?"

"I don't want to go," Sophie whispered.

Marc-Emmanuel read the letter again, with its "dear little
aeronaute" and "my sweet shred of silk," but the message
was clear. Napoleon wanted his official balloonist to fly him
over the prospective battlefields in Austria. Duroc was to escort her.

Marc-Emmanuel sent Sophie's acceptance tower to tower
to Strasbourg, where it was picked up by courier and carried
across Austria to Vienna.

"Merveilleux!" Napoleon flagged back.

Marc-Emmanuel could hear the r's rolling in delight.

He dispatched a letter to Isabelle. Sophie must have a chaperone, and who better than a mother to protect her daughter from an emperor's advances? Marc-Emmanuel couldn't believe his good fortune. Under normal circumstances, the ritual of mourning would have prevented his seeing Isabelle for some time.

In Vienna, in the Schoenbrunn Palace when Marc-Emmauel, Sophie, and Isabelle approached the emperor's chambers, they heard his cries of pain.

"What in hell are you doing?" Napoleon shouted. "You are sitting on top of the Danube!"

"I am not. I am—"

"You are sitting like a duck shitting in the Danube!"

"No, I am *not*, emperor. Do you not see—"

"How can I see anything when you are taking up half of Austria? Move over into France!"

The group outside the door looked at one another, mystified, until Méneval emerged to say that the emperor and his cartographer were crawling around the floor on a large-scale map of the battlefield where they often bumped heads. Then Napoleon came out in a rumpled shirt and a stained white waistcoat, rubbing his forehead, with his hair disheveled and looking like a family man up just from his Sunday nap.

Like any proud new homeowner, he gave his guests a partial tour of the bright yellow fourteen-hundred-room palace, then showed them to their quarters. Though they pretended to take no note, to some the placement of their rooms was of the greatest interest. It was early when the travelers retired after dinner and not much later when there was a knock at Isabelle's door.

"I hope I have not come too soon," said Marc-Emmanuel.

The next day, seeing Isabelle and Marc-Emmanuel walk in to breakfast together, Napoleon didn't snigger like a schoolboy as he would ordinarily.

He bent respectfully over the widow Armant's hand.

Looking at her mother, Sophie understood. Isabelle had been fond of her father, but she had never flushed with pleasure at seeing him or let a hand fall to his shoulder. The calm with which her mother nourished the family had not come from love for him.

Meanwhile Napoleon, a cup of coffee in one hand, was trying to smooth Sophie's hair. He jumped up and offered her a tray of pastries.

"Your Highness, this is unnecessary! I can be served by another," Sophie said.

"By none so well as one who lives to serve you!" said Napoleon.

"Others have been trained to it," Sophie said as he spilled his coffee on the damask cloth.

"But they have not my enthusiasm for the task!"

"In this instance enthusiasm surpasses skill," said Sophie as they smiled at each other. As Napoleon, dithering, shook out her napkin and spread it carefully on her lap.

Mon Dieu! Marc-Emmanuel said to himself.

Then the emperor discussed his war plan. He had

been badly beaten by the Austrians earlier in May, and the next battle was all important, Napoleon said. He wished Sophie to escort him over the terrain. Though in fact the emperor's problem seemed insoluble. The Danube lay between him and the enemy. To achieve victory thousands of French soldiers had to land on the far bank nearly at the same time.

Napoleon saw Sophie hesitating. "Fewer men will die if the battle is well conceived," he said. "The wind is high and from the northwest. The balloon is ready."

He tossed his napkin on the table and stood.

The night before, Méneval had told Sophie the emperor grieved for a friend wounded fatally that spring. In a surgeon's tent Bonaparte had held Marshal Lannes in his arms and wept. Since then he always wore the white cashmere waistcoat stained with his dead friend's blood.

Sophie had been moved by the story. She didn't know yet that it was as necessary for Napoleon to order death on the battlefield as it was for him to grieve over it.

She stood too.

Napoleon hummed tunelessly as they rolled smoothly along the Ringstrasse. He had just decided to divorce Joséphine and it amused him (as it hadn't before) to recall his wife's fear of carriages. If he had told her once, he had told her a thousand times, "An empress must have courage!"

He looked at Sophie—that very quality made flesh!—and noticed she had mended the skirt of her black dress not in

one place but several. Napoleon stopped humming. One of
Sophie's attractions was her simplicity. Joséphine had just
had a dress made of toucan feathers that cost the empire
forty-seven thousand francs, and another of fresh rose petals,
hand sewn. Even so.

"You mustn't give away all of your money!" he scolded. "I
will have to buy you a new dress."

Looking down at the pockets she had made to hold her
coins, Sophie didn't see the long line of wounded French
soldiers outside St. Stephen's Hospital.

Within an hour she and the emperor were gazing at the
only balloon Méneval was able to find, an old red one that
belonged to an aging local count. "It is pretty unusual as balloons go," Méneval had said. "Winters are hard in Austria,
and the count designed an outer covering in order to shake
off the snow." Sophie studied the device, which involved a
second set of lines; Jean-Pierre had designed something simi-
lar when he had dreamed of flying over the arctic—one *sure*
way to fame! he had said. Sophie checked the knots that held
the covering like a shawl around a woman's head, then signaled to Napoleon to climb aboard.

Given the emperor's inclination to seasickness anything
was possible. But he was boisterous as a boy, fiddling with
the lines and hanging playfully over the side. "You must be a
high floater," Sophie said. In the tidal pool as a child she had
bobbed like a shorebird, and she sometimes thought she was
at ease in the air because she was more buoyant than most.
Napoleon hesitated. Sophie had made *high floater* sound like a

compliment. "In the Bay of Ajaccio, I was like a cork from a bottle of Chianti!" he bragged.

But as they crossed the Danube, he was all business, looking for places to hide four pontoon bridges. When they reached the far side of the river, he searched the flat plain for the slightest rise or depression where his soldiers could take cover.

At the same time Napoleon was aware of Sophie's body only inches from his. Others might have been disappointed in the view of her from the side, but he wanted to lose himself in the subtle rises and depressions that lifted and fell along it. He wanted to take her to Odiot's to have a tiny silver cup made that only he would drink from. Below, a small white birch tree reminded him of Sophie, and he longed to run his hand down her white back. He loved her straight spine because he wanted to bend it.

Sophie knew Napoleon was intent on her. In the little boat at Malmaison, his kisses had had a formal quality; like an engraved invitation, they had required only a limited response. But now his white shirt was open at the throat and he had rolled up his sleeves. Whenever he turned in the basket, his arms brushed against hers.

Sophie's heart was beating unevenly again, a moth's wing fluttering too near a flame, when a rogue wind drove into their current. Part of the balloon's red outer shell came loose and Sophie saw Napoleon through scarlet-colored silk. His waistcoat looked newly bloodied and so did his hands as they gestured to a crimson battlefield. Though she had heard talk of hundreds of thousands of soldiers dying under Napoleon's command, she had not understood until now. Seeing him smile, she knew he had solved the problem of the coming battle.

Shaken, Sophie knotted the covering back in place. But the wind grew stronger. The balloon stretched alarmingly as the airship careened between parallel currents like a sailboat heeling between two tacks. Napoleon moved quickly at her instruction, opening the top vent and tightening the lines while she lashed the outer covering more securely.

At last the balloon was stable, but they were silent for the rest of the flight.

From time to time, Napoleon had toyed with the idea of using airships as forward observers. In 1794 a balloon factory had been up and running in Meudon, turning out spheres that sported names like *Heaven* and *Céleste* and were piloted by an aerial combat unit of twenty uniformed men. In Fréjus, using a few of the airships to signal enemy troop movements to the nearest semaphore tower, General Jourdan had won a battle against the Austrians.

But after this ride the emperor never mentioned the subject of ballooning again.

Soon they landed safely and were ferried back across the Danube. This time, riding through Vienna at twilight, Sophie wasn't looking down as they passed the maimed French soldiers waiting in front of St. Stephen's Hospital.

Noticing her tremor, Napoleon asked if she was cold.

The moment they arrived at the Schoenbrunn Palace,

Sophie drew Marc-Emmanuel aside. "Of course those battle-fields will be awash in blood!" he told her. "Kléber said Napoleon consumes six thousand soldiers a day! I'd say more. After all, the army's chief surgeon didn't have a single bandage when the last battle began, and food for the wounded was cooked in pots hammered from the armor of dead soldiers."

That night at dinner Napoleon drank only tea. But when he tossed and turned in bed it wasn't because he was feeling sick. It was because his empire required a royal marriage and a royal heir, and he knew Sophie would never consent to live as his mistress in a cottage outside Paris.

Sophie lay awake too, unable to make sense of the fact that Napoleon was as happy on a battlefield as in a garden.

The next morning, Isabelle was relieved to see that nothing kept her daughter in Vienna any longer, though she thought Sophie and the emperor seemed comfortable with each other. Her daughter was calm and he had put on a clean white waistcoat.

Napoleon's torment was made plain only on parting.

Standing at the entrance to the palace, he said a gallant good-bye complete with white-gloved mock salute and click of polished boots. Impassive, he saw Isabelle handed into the waiting carriage. But when Marc-Emmanuel turned next to Sophie, Napoleon threw down his bicorne and stamped on it. Running across the courtyard, his spurs scattering pebbles, he kicked at them and scattered more until he reached her. He grabbed her shoulders and pushed them back like a soldier's, swept his hand straight as a plumb line down her spine, then walked away.

He did not watch as the coachman flicked the reins and Sophie, Isabelle, and Marc-Emmanuel set off for France.

Constant walked slowly upstairs to get another hat.

24

A FRIEND STEPS IN

MARC-EMMANUEL WAS SURE OF THREE THINGS. First, it was obvious Sophie would not wait forever for André; second, the misunderstanding between the two was so complete as to have assumed the heft of truth; and third, a balloon was an excellent place to address such difficulties because escape was impossible.

After arranging with Sophie to take him for a balloon ride the next afternoon, Marc-Emmanuel set off along the Seine. Just past the broad steps leading up to the Château of St. Cloud he crossed the bridge to Boulogne. In front of André's farmhouse a dock needed repair and an old rowboat was pulled up onshore; from the back Marc-Emmanuel heard the sounds of a man swearing and an ax striking wood.

"I'm a peasant boy, but my hands weren't made for this," André said by way of greeting as he tossed a pair of split logs in the air and caught them with a deftness that belied his words.

He looked rested, a bit heavier and bigger somehow, Marc-Emmanuel thought. But still. "You have *nearly* lost her."

"Sophie hasn't been mine to lose since she was a child."

Marc-Emmanuel was aware that some aspect of the man eluded him. For a moment he thought of the old corporal's refrain, that it was André's life, after all. But still. "You *will* lose her if you don't act now," Marc-Emmanuel said, though he resisted the temptation to reassure André that Sophie didn't love Napoleon. The young fellow had a prickly arrogance and didn't take kindly to anything smacking of condescension. Instead Marc-Emmanuel asked about his move to the old corporal's farmhouse.

"Such a good fellow," André said. "He's given it to me, won't take a sou for it. Says he's happier living with his sister." André lived on such offerings though rarely so large as this; most people were too poor to give, but others contributed generously to his work.

An hour later Marc-Emmanuel sat alone in the courtyard of an inn. André had said nothing about Sophie when they said good-bye. Out of pride, he suspected. His head ached. The doors to the courtyard were closed and all around him echoed the sounds of horseshoes hitting stone. Isabelle would be disappointed the visit had not gone well. Marc-Emmanuel got a bottle of Cognac from the inn and unbuttoned his waistcoat.

The next morning he hadn't even finished his coffee when André rode into the courtyard.

"Best get started, don't you think?" André was grinning.

"I didn't think you would come!"

"I just wanted to give you a scare!" In truth, André had gotten little sleep. He didn't relish riding to Sophie only to find her in love with Napoleon, but he was damned if he would ask that busybody Marc-Emmanuel what was going on!

He hadn't slept because pride was a hard bed.

Together André and Marc-Emmanuel galloped along the Seine, and when they saw the top of a balloon above the trees they turned down a path in the Bois de Boulogne. "There's not enough champagne and foie gras for three," Marc-Emmanuel said breezily as he untied a picnic basket and handed it to one of the workmen. "Anyway, the balloon is too small. I'm off."

But watching Sophie and André, he sighed.

They had scarcely glanced at each other. Sophie moved as if she were invisibly weighted, and André looked stern. The handlers were toying with the lines; it was past two, past time for them to eat. Finally Sophie gestured and when one of them lifted her into the basket, André swung over the side.

Marc-Emmanuel cantered up the path and didn't look back.

Sophie was sure that the boy she loved was gone and that the man he had become was here only at Marc-Emmanuel's insistence. So be it! she thought. Dropping sandbags over the side, she flew them into a mist so thick it left their faces wet. She carved an arc on a high curving wind and spun over the tops of clouds, then languished in a slow current.

André was glad for the distraction, and marveled at the

secrets hidden in transparent air, its hidden updrafts and floes of cold. At sunset he saw gold glaze Sophie's cheeks and tangle in her hair. But as the colors on the ponds below began to fade, he brooded on the night Napoleon had stroked her arm. "Have you lost your fear of carriages yet?" André said at last. "The newspapers say you are afraid to ride in one."

"There is no escape from carriages," Sophie said. "They are everywhere in Paris."

"Especially when someone sends one for you."

Sophie adjusted a valve on the vent overhead.

"Especially when the emperor of France sends a carriage for you, is that not so?"

"I am not his mistress."

"But no, of *course* not! How could you be? After all, you took your *mother* along when Napoleon invited you to Vienna!"

When Sophie reached up again to readjust the valve, André moved his hand quickly along her arm, sensation running through him as weightless and compelling as the memory of her had been for years.

He traced her body lightly, then looked away.

Sophie's heart fell when André's hand slipped past places where it might have paused. At first she thought that, like Jean-Pierre, he was disappointed at finding rocky ground, and so she busied herself with unpacking their picnic.

Then she thought again. "You believe I am in love with Napoleon."

"How can I not? Your feet were *bare!*"

"They were in stockings and they were wet."

"That makes no difference!"

"When Jean-Pierre died, you didn't write," Sophie said calmly.

"Because within the week I saw you in Napoleon's bedroom!"

"Still, you didn't try."

There was silence. André filled it by opening the champagne.

"I thought you no longer cared," he said finally.

"I too," Sophie said. "I thought you no longer cared."

Their words were their future, but for a moment Sophie was unsure. For years she had imagined André's hand on her and she could call up his face more quickly than she could her own. Now he was so near, she didn't recognize the angle of his jaw or the shock of his black hair. The parts of his face she saw seemed large and indistinct, like words in Jean-Pierre's magnifying glass.

They could belong to anyone, Sophie thought.

Until he touched her.

An hour later, when they landed in a moonlit valley just outside a village, André saw the gleam of Sophie's skin on her collarbone and the small blue vein beating at her temple. He had loved these signs of the structure beneath her skin since he was a boy, and so it startled him when emotion overtook the pleasure of finally putting a hand to what he had longed to touch. Then life as he knew it slid away, for the healing in his hands turned to passion, and his body carried him farther than understanding could. Later in the lantern light, seeing the faint outline of Sophie's bones fine-knit as a bird's wing beneath thin translucent skin, he wanted only to pin her to earth and him.

At dawn when she opened her eyes, Sophie thought André's arms around her were fragments of a dream, like a wisp of moon in the morning sky. She fell back asleep and when she woke again, the arms were gone.

Soon André appeared, carrying a baguette and a pail of café au lait, but Sophie couldn't be consoled. She cried for all the years they had been apart, for all the years she had not allowed herself to cry. Taking her in his arms, he sang her favorite lullaby of a boy urging a shepherd girl to come and live with him.

"Don't you see?" said André. "It's come true."

25

THREE COUPLES

AT FIRST IT SEEMED AS if it would take time for Sophie and André to get used to each other, but they accomplished it in a day.

On rue Cassette, when Sophie led him up the stairs, within minutes André was tearing Jean-Pierre's balloon from the walls. "If I must—to have you—I will live in another man's house," he said. "But I will not sit in his balloon!"

Soon the floor of the salon was awash in blue silk.

In the kitchen, over a supper of bread and cheese, he raised his glass and said, "To Marc-Emmanuel, without him there would be no wedding!"

"We don't need to take any vows," said Sophie, slicing more bread. "A thread of memories already binds us."

"A thread of *what*?" André put down his glass. As he ran his hands through his hair, he saw Sophie blush.

Then he laughed and reached across the table to tap her cheek.

"A marriage vow would take away that blush. Evidently a mere *thread* cannot!"

Later Sophie smiled, hearing him swear. He was fixing her chimney flue. When they were children and a bolt or latch had refused to yield, he had flared then too. She had thought it was from impatience, but over time she decided it was more than that.

One day she had asked him.

"I have no time to waste," André had said when he was still young.

Now he pulled on his boots and tucked in his shirt. "I'm going to check on the barn. I have the key."

And was gone.

Skidding across the silk floor, Sophie threw open the casement windows that had been covered by Jean-Pierre's balloon and watched André until he was out of sight.

At midnight she was asleep beneath a comforter when he walked into the bedroom and sat down on her.

As Sophie struggled out from under him, he stared.

"How am I to know you are lying in a bed if it is as flat as a crêpe?" he teased.

Taking her outstretched arms in his, he kissed her and said, "How can you have carnal thoughts when you have no flesh?"

For days, on entering the room, André asked the bed quite formally if anyone was in it.

Sophie was undone by joy.

She burned things in pots and forgot to latch the door. She

stared vacantly out the window. When people spoke she smiled, sometimes when it would have been better had she not, at the news of a neighbor's sick cat. Setting off quickly up the stairs, she wondered at the top what she was doing there.

And so, in slightly slapdash fashion, Sophie and André came to live famously together on rue Cassette.

A beautiful woman in Napoleon's court might have the admiration of the entire entourage, and a fashionable Parisienne wearing the latest gown and rolling down St. Honoré in an open carriage might be the talk of the day's drive, but Sophie sailing over the farms and villages of France was known to everyone. And when people learned that a gifted young healer had won her heart, André began to be as celebrated. In part this was because he was something of a romantic figure. Some women, particularly those on the mend, were inclined to mistake his intensity for desire, and so they wanted to see him often. Others who weren't ill at all came away feeling faint, their breathing uneven, and this, too, required further attention.

At all hours couriers rang with invitations for Sophie to ascend in fetes. Others came with pleas to André written by people with pressing needs. Sometimes narrow little rue Cassette was so crowded with admirers that carriages couldn't get through.

"We will be puffed up with pride if we stay here one second longer," André said one day, pulling out a trunk. "I think we should move to my farmhouse in Boulogne."

Sophie put on a wine-colored dress. Then she took it off and chose a red one with a very low neck.

She adjusted a hat carefully in the mirror.

She handed André his best frock coat. "Let's celebrate at the Grand Véfour!"

In the restaurant the thousand mirrors conceived to indulge lovers only confirmed Sophie and André's fame, for their faces were reflected countless times. "I couldn't help but notice you," Daguerre told Sophie as he walked up to their table with a girl on his arm. "You are stunning under a wide black brim."

Sophie smiled at him. "This is nearly the first time I've seen you on your feet!"

"Louise and I have just spent a pleasant morning at Cusset's ordering the silk for her wedding gown," said Daguerre, kissing Sophie's hand.

André nodded coolly as the waiters brought chairs.

"It is so nice, finally, to meet some of Mandé's friends," Louise said warmly. "He spends every spare moment thinking about how to fix sunlight on a piece of metal! Do you suppose he's mad?"

"I was forced to tell her my whole name when she said she would marry me," said Louis Jacques Mandé Daguerre. "Though I worry she can't grasp the ambition typical of some poor boys."

"You have only to think of Napoleon," André told Louise.

Daguerre laughed. "Now, *that's* the kind of fame I crave!"

As they left, in the flurry of good-byes Sophie invited them to dinner on Christmas Eve.

"How do you know him?" André asked Sophie later.

She looked at him quickly. "André, Daguerre is nine years younger than I am!"

"So what? Marc-Emmanuel is ten years younger than your mother!"

He looked sheepish but he couldn't laugh.

The only time André was angry with Sophie was when he was jealous.

That evening in another part of Paris an unlikely troupe set off. Joséphine and two of her favorite mongrels, along with their litters of puppies and a parrot in a cage, left Fontainebleau, followed by carriages piled high with trunks and hatboxes. Two weeks before, at the end of a dinner that had lasted ten silent minutes, Napoleon announced he was proceeding with a divorce.

"Malmaison is yours," he told Joséphine. "Plant whatever you want."

Moments later she had begun crying hysterically and together Napoleon and the prefect of the palace, Count Bausette, had carried her to her apartments.

"You are holding me too tight!" she had whispered to the count.

But her little ploy hadn't worked and Joséphine's marriage was at an end. At the pretty country house the carriage doors were opened, and as the dogs and their puppies were carried off along with the rasping parrot, an Egyptian gazelle in Joséphine's little zoo pricked up its ears at the sounds of the new arrivals.

"Malmaison, *c'est Joséphine,*" Napoleon would say in the years to come, the two inseparable in his mind. He always smiled at the thought of her flowers spilling onto the paths and bursting over every fence and wall erected to restrain them; Joséphine didn't like corsets either.

Within weeks Sophie and André were unpacking plates and furniture in his farmhouse in Boulogne. Crates were everywhere when her mother and Marc-Emmanuel arrived the day before Christmas, but Sophie had managed to decorate the farmhouse for the holiday. In the tradition of her childhood, she had filled bowls with grapes and around the windows she had put up laurel branches strung with apples and pears.

Cracking walnuts for a cake, Sophie told stories about the creatures in André's care—about the dove that lived in the kitchen and seemed well enough but refused to fly. She talked about the little pig with the wound on his forehead that had keeled over in fright when her basket had swung against a barn in Strasbourg, though she didn't add she had been afraid in the air that day, and several other times in recent months. When she had dropped into the farmyard and seen the frightened pig, its fear seemed to mirror hers, and she had asked the farmer to let her take it home.

Later that afternoon Cusset arrived from Lyon and set about hanging the silk curtains he had brought. "The color of fresh-churned butter," he said proudly. "Perfect for a farmhouse!"

As André ambled through the house with his shirttails out, looking in boxes for candles, and Sophie called to him, they seemed like any couple getting ready for a family party.

But an hour later, after separating in Boulogne to do last-minute Christmas errands, their eyes raked the village. André scowled as he searched the market for the small, sharp wing of her shoulder and Sophie looked in every corner of the square for sign of him. When they found each other, their arms filled with oranges and candles, they smiled, almost in surprise.

That evening Daguerre and Louise arrived from Paris and they unwrapped a crèche he had made. "I'm a set designer after all!" he said, carefully arranging the manger and the an-imals on the mantel.

André brought in a gnarled piece of oak he had set aside months before; oak was a dense wood and he knew the log would burn for hours. It was his *bûche de Noël*. In his weeks spent splitting wood and trying not to think of Sophie, his choice of a Yule log had been the only sign of hope he had al-lowed himself that things might come out right. As he watched it begin to catch, André didn't know he was hum-ming, but Sophie heard him and began to sing.

Listening to everyone join in, it occurred to Marc-Emmanuel that most of them, like him, had lost relatives in the war; then he sang too.

A few days after Christmas, when Marc-Emmanuel and Is-abelle had returned to Beaune and the maid had brought them tea, he said, "I am going to read you to sleep. I found this in the box of books you brought from La Salière—Rousseau's letters to a young woman. A lover, I gather, though I'm told he had more than one." Leafing past an etching of a small man with black, springy hair, Marc-Emmanuel said, "This was written in 1776: 'Gatekeeper of my heart, let no one pass but you. Your kiss seals my heart shut tight against another as any key!'"

Isabelle smiled, remembering her visit as a girl to friends in Montmorency, where she had met Rousseau.

Marc-Emmanuel turned the page. "'It was good of you to take my cat. You will remember, she likes to sleep beneath the bed.'" He looked up in surprise. "Why, that's what your cats do!"

But Isabelle was drifting off to sleep. Because of Rousseau, at twenty she had left her forbidding childhood home. With his gray-striped cat in her arms and his child on the way, she had walked away forever from La Rochelle.

"'Enchanting child, mistress of my heart, I will weave gold and silver threads and make the ribbons for your wedding cap,'" Marc-Emmanuel read. "'My dear green girl, would the groom were me!'"

When he blew out the candle and Isabelle reached for him, the cat curled under their bed didn't stir.

26

ON THE BANKS OF
THE SEINE

IN ST. CLOUD THAT JANUARY, Napoleon was refurbishing his favorite château for his fiancée, Marie-Louise, the daughter of the Austrian king. Sophie and André heard the emperor had grown fat since his narrow victory in Austria and had retreated from society even more, attending to each detail of his bride's trousseau, ordering all manner of dresses and lingerie, everything to be made from the very finest, whitest silk. And what did Napoleon think when he saw his sturdy red-cheeked princess decked out in her delicate finery?

"I need a womb," said the forty-one-year-old emperor.

Besides, he couldn't annex Russia until he had annexed all of Austria. If he didn't, what would he hitch Russia *to*? The logic of conquest was childishly simple.

The village of St. Cloud swarmed with workmen as the renovations continued apace.

.   .   .

Across the bridge in Boulogne, André and Sophie lived simply. A maid was supposed to cook and clean, but often she forgot and so did they. Sometimes their copper tub was littered with bits of grass and other small leavings of a briefly wounded duck or hedgehog, and when the neighborhood children stopped by they nudged each other for a look at the latest creature in the bath.

Because of his years living alone, André was surprised by the complexity of domestic life. As she had when she was young, from time to time Sophie sat on his lap and confided the secrets of her day, then asked for his. But some mornings he woke to an unfamiliar and languorous Sophie who wouldn't get out of bed. When he stood up and pulled on his breeches, she took his pillows and piled them behind her. Taking no notice of him, she brushed her hair until it floated like a dark cloud behind her face. Then, putting a hand to her hip, she arched her back and pretended to stretch.

André knew Sophie's gestures were as calculated as any he could imagine, but they still drove him back to bed.

Often, it seemed to him that he was caught unaware.

Sophie might spend a morning preparing something she had eaten once in Milan, thin-sliced veal with a lemon sauce that she remembered with pleasure, and dinner would be formal. But another day, walking home, he might see her bustling about outside, spreading a cloth on the wall down by the Seine and setting out bread and cheese. While he was in the house getting a bottle of wine, she might ask a neighbor passing by on the towpath to join them.

.   .   .

One morning Sophie was making a cassoulet with white beans she had bought in Strasbourg.

At her feet was the dove that would not fly. When a winter rain started to fall, the bird walked out the open door, clambered to the top of a low root cellar, and slid down the wet, mossy roof. Watching it climb back up, then shoot down the slick slope again, Sophie decided that only fear could tie to earth a being meant to fly.

Why else would it play such a game, and choose safety over flight?

At dinner the rain fell faster and wind whipped across the Seine.

"What is it?" Sophie asked.

André was studying the fast-running current on the river and the rowboat he had tied securely to the dock.

"Landfall," he said softly as he turned to her.

In Lyon a few weeks later, in a bedroom of Cusset's house, Sophie waited for André. He was to heal in a cathedral the next morning and she had an early ascent.

It was late when André arrived, and he and Cusset made no sound as they walked through the richly appointed house. Upstairs in the candlelit bedroom the colors in the Aubusson rug caught the light and the tables shone.

André leaned against the closed door with his hands on his hips.

There was a luster to the carved mahogany bed and to her.

"Your collar is torn," Sophie said sleepily.

"I couldn't find the maid."

"Here there are many maids and no grass in the tub."

"More to the point, no gray-striped cat playing under the bed," said André, unbuttoning his shirt.

The next morning, even though the air was light and she ascended slowly, Sophie was frightened. As Jean-Pierre once had, she gripped the basket and kept her eyes on land. Looking down at the Cathedral of St. Jean, she saw the line of people waiting to see André. Then she smiled. He had come to the door, and as they waved to each other, suddenly she realized that her fear of carriages had begun with the one that had wheeled her from him years ago, just as the balloon had taken her from him now.

Sophie looked up at the vent. She would wait ten minutes then open the valve.

Perhaps it wasn't possible to want to fly only partway up the sky, she thought.

Perhaps it wasn't possible to be only partly free.

In the cathedral André lost his concentration precisely at noon. On the clock above him a metal rooster screeched twelve times, as it and other barnyard animals enacted the Annunciation.

"It happens almost every hour until after four o'clock," whispered the woman limping up. "You'll get used to it."

André nodded and tried not to think how Sophie would laugh.

He tried to concentrate on the woman leaning on her cane.

At the end of the morning's healing, André walked into

Cusset's workroom. Sophie had just arrived, and turning quickly at the sound of his voice, she brushed against a table as he reached out his hand for the bottle when it fell.

"A *rooster?*" she said.

"Among others," André said, tightening the cork and setting the bottle of varnish well back from the edge.

"The animals are on a fourteenth-century astronomical clock," Cusset told Sophie. "It chimes a hymn at the same time the cock crows."

"It is a mad scene and it makes a hell of a noise," said André.

At four o'clock they were standing in front of the raucous little menagerie.

"I'm homesick," she said, surprising him.

On place de la Baleine, after she ordered her trunk sent on to Boulogne, André swung Sophie in front of him on his black mare, and as he held her they smiled, each thinking of the day in Sancerre when he had been on horseback and she had flown away from him over the hills.

In St. Cloud Napoleon was organizing every minute of his wedding to Marie-Louise and their solemn entry into Paris on April 2. To make sure the citizenry erupted in goodwill, he ordered huge vats of wine along with quantities of chickens, geese, and legs of lamb to be placed in different parts of the city. The centerpiece of the celebration—the diamond in his crown—was to be Sophie in a balloon ascending before him in the Tuileries Gardens, and that

morning Napoleon dispatched his secretary to the farmhouse in Boulogne.

By chance Méneval knocked at the door on André's birth-
day. But in spite of the festive mood—over champagne they
toasted the fact that the three of them would turn thirty-two
that year—Sophie didn't reply when Méneval made the emperor's request. Remembering the battlefield she had seen
outside of Vienna and the thousands of soldiers who had
died at Wagram, she asked Méneval if she could have a word
with the emperor.

André was sure this was out of some lingering affection for
Napoleon, that the coming marriage was cause for regret on
Sophie's part. At the end of the afternoon when she called to
him to come and say good-bye to Méneval, he turned away.

The next day Sophie walked up the steps of Napoleon's
château. Here is not the wild release of Malmaison, she
thought. A groundsman told her the emperor had ordered
everything manicured and the lawns made sleek. "Think of
it," he said. "The emperor is even regulating the size and
number of swans!"

Napoleon was standing in a reception room before the fire.

"I will no longer fly for the emperor of France," Sophie
told him.

Napoleon studied her.

"Do only this," he said, and finally she nodded.

When she left, Napoleon kicked a log and sent sparks
flying.

Such courage!

And he had thought he couldn't love her more!

Two weeks later Sophie returned to the château to be fitted for her gown. Servants guided her to a dressing room where Napoleon appeared, followed by Cusset.

To her surprise, Goethe also entered the room.

"Madame Blanchard," he said in his warm voice and bad French, bending over her hand. "Some assume I have come to attend the emperor's wedding and others, that I want to discuss with Monsieur Cusset how to make my theater curtain fall with authority. I am really here to inquire if your balloons are behaving themselves."

"I hope my spheres rise as quickly as your curtains fall, monsieur."

"Cusset tells me my curtain needs leading in the hem, that weight is necessary for silk to descend swiftly," said Goethe.

Sophie smiled. "Mine is the opposite challenge."

Napoleon glowered at Goethe and gestured to Sophie to go and dress.

They were silent when she stood before them, for her gown appeared to be not one color but all colors combined. It is silk's natural shade, Cusset told them. Lustrous and pearly, it reflects different facets where light falls. Taking a spool of thin cording with white feathers woven through it, Cusset cut a length and pinned it to Sophie's skirt.

Of course Napoleon couldn't resist. He grabbed the box of pins and tried to fit her dress more tightly. He poked her here and there, and when she cried he swore. As usual, the servants sweated and poured coffee. The seamstress poked her finger with a needle and it bled on several feathers. Duplan wasn't there to wave his hands about, but still, everyone was worn out when they finally stopped to look.

After a moment Goethe stepped forward and removed the feathered thread from her skirt. The night before, waking from a dream, he had run to a desk and written a single line, then gone back to bed. Now he smiled as he pinned a tracery of white feathers to Sophie's small shoulder blades. The meaning of the words he had written down were still a mystery to him, but the figure in his dream no longer was.

Napoleon hung his head.

Only for an empire would he have given up such an angel!

"I remember," Sophie said to Goethe with a smile as the emperor gritted his teeth. "Your grandfather was a tailor!"

Goethe and Cusset walked with Sophie across the bridge and down the towpath to the farmhouse. "My scientist friends tell me Lamarck is slowly going blind, did you know?" Goethe said.

"No. I sent him the charts he wanted, but I never heard from him. I suppose that's why."

Seeing her tremble slightly, Goethe took her arm. "Lamarck was the first to catalog the clouds," he said gently. "The very first, in 1801. That's more than most people accomplish in a lifetime of sight."

Marc-Emmanuel stood with André in the doorway of the farmhouse, genial as ever. He had been in Paris on business and had driven to Boulogne with Daguerre and Louise. As he sometimes did, he would spend the night before going on to Beaune.

While Sophie mixed the eggs and sliced the truffles for omelets, Louise made a salad.

"I worry about Mandé," said Louise. "He spends all of his time thinking about how to capture the present and not a minute enjoying it."

As she set the table, Sophie remembered how Daguerre had wanted to capture the sight of a white cloth and a bowl of Stephanotis at Cusset's dinner party. He was possessed by the idea of preserving the moment for all time, like Lamarck in his attic room, gripped by the possibility of catologing the clouds. "Daguerre has set himself a task," Sophie told Louise. "There is joy in that."

Over supper Goethe and Cusset discussed the problem of torque in an elongated sphere. Goethe was surprised it didn't occur more often and Cusset explained that silk has twenty percent elasticity, that it could stretch to accommodate a moderate lateral wind and still snap back to its original shape. André paled at the fragility of flight. He drank a glass of Merlot quickly and said no matter what, a round sphere sounds safer. Goethe began to work out the measurements and Daguerre drew a little sketch, but Sophie displayed no interest in the new design.

She was watching André pour a second glass of wine.

When he got up to open another bottle, she pulled him to her.

On the day of the emperor's wedding celebration in Paris, when the clouds rolled away at last, the procession shone.

SOPHIE'S ASCENSION AT NAPOLEON'S WEDDING
CELEBRATION, CHAMP-DE-MARS, 1810

Napoleon had a knack for designing uniforms and medals, and the thousands of Imperial Guardsmen flashing by made an impressive display. But their numbers couldn't compensate for the fact that twenty-one bright red cardinals had failed to show up. A mistake. Napoleon would banish the absentees— first to prison for a year or two and then into black robes forever.

Across France to commemorate the day: thousands of gold and silver medallions of the bridal couple distributed, thousands of dowries for worthy daughters given out, and thousands of church bells rung, all accomplished in the spirit of generosity—and unity with Austria.

Later Napoleon remembered little of that. He remembered only the celestial figure rising before him.

Floating above the emperor and his bride, Sophie recalled her own wedding day when a carriage had wheeled her from the boy she loved. It had made her fearful, being separated from André. As she was fearful, leaving him now.

But suddenly she was struck by the difference between choosing to be in a balloon and being compelled to ride in a carriage.

No one—not even Napoleon—was forcing her to ascend.

Sophie narrowed her eyes; if ever she chose not to fly, it would be on better grounds than fear.

27

LANDFALL

FOR THREE DAYS early that spring an ice storm froze the villages southwest of Paris.

Sunlight danced along the vines on the old farmhouse and turned it into a curvaceous folly. When she stepped outside to look the first morning, Sophie fell and twisted her left ankle. André noted ruefully that the swelling subsided as soon as he touched it, his love was so completely hers. Though she limped only slightly, when the sun had burned through the ice on the towpath enough to soften it, he clasped her firmly and fitted his right hip against her left side. Then he laughed. *"Prends un abri bergère, à ma droite, en marchant!"* he sang. He held her so close, Sophie heard the old lullaby, which invited a shepherd girl to take shelter walking at his right side, echo in his chest.

Then André shortened his stride to match hers and they walked along the Seine. A sheen of ice shone on all of Boulogne. The houses and trees glittered in the sun like just-cut glass and even the iced-over surfaces of worn-out things—old hoes, pails, and axes—were shot through with sparkling particles of many-colored light.

A coiled rope hanging on a barn door was rimed into a blazing wreath.

It was brighter out than any summer day and people were giddy at the sight of transparency everywhere. Crystal edges disappeared into light and nothing seemed solid. Even the walls of barns looked as if they could be walked through.

Sophie smiled. In the years before she and André had found each other again, she had searched out the fastest winds, hoping to slip through a crevice into the light-filled realm she had once glimpsed. The sky has finally shattered, she thought, and what lies beyond it is this shining, translucent world.

Every night the melting ice froze and not even the smallest branch could move. The windows and doors of the farmhouses were sealed shut and it was warm inside as Boulogne waited for the next bright day.

When the ice finally melted into spring, Sophie decided to complete a task she had put off. Months before, the scientists at the National Institute of Arts and Sciences had asked her to ascend and she had hesitated out of fear.

Now, just beyond Boulogne, she shot up on a powerful wind.

But though she was hurtling through space, her sense of stillness was complete, for she was in mist. Always before, she had liked to watch the sun shine across the surfaces of things. But today no brightness silvered the tops of clouds. It diffused through them from the north, glowing and consistent, and she found a different beauty in the deeper light; like her mother's calm, it seemed to come from within.

Sophie wanted little lateral distance in her climb up the sky because her hydrogen would last longer if she rose quickly. But soaring and tacking among fast-rising winds meant she had to work quickly. First she positioned her new thermometer and barometer, for they were bulky and difficult to maneuver. Then, as she dropped sandbags over the side, she wrapped herself in a heavy wool cloak and placed a board across the basket to use as a writing table. She made note of each half degree change in temperature and any accompanying movement of the mercury in her barometer. By taking both into account, scientists could estimate the altitudes she attained; at times she had done it herself. But soon, even without calculating her height in the air, when she darted through a hole in a cloud bank and into a clear sky, Sophie was certain she was higher than she had ever been before. On other flights she had gotten cold and tired. Now she felt faint and was gasping for air.

After making her last notations, Sophie began her descent. Tomorrow she would write the scientists that if she were bundled in fur robes and riding in a roofed-in basket, she could pilot an airship even higher.

And that she would try, if she were willing to risk her heart no longer beating.

Sophie was smiling as she fell asleep.

Already her flight had the warmth of memory, a hint of nostalgia, for she had taken leave of the sky.

In Boulogne several hours later, Sophie ran into the barn.

"What is it?" André asked in astonishment. On her face was a blaze of feeling, so great that it was nearly of light.

"Landfall," Sophie said, smiling as he caught the bit of bright silk that was slipping from her shoulders. She had found a better reason than fear not to fly.

Until now the wonder had been that finally Sophie and André held what they had loved since they were young, and that their bodies had become as familiar as the beach stones they used to fit into the palms of their hands. But that night they were blind to flesh and bone, without memory. And they were insistent, as if each emotion could be unearthed, and known.

The next morning, sitting on the terrace, though their mood was lighter, André and Sophie were more open than was usual for them. "You have told me that in Jean-Pierre you found the freedom of flight," he said. "What have you found in me?" He was grinning, for he was sure he knew.

But Sophie was solemn. "You. I found you."

As the lazy maid bestirred herself to bring them coffee, Sophie watched a family of ducks waddle down to the Seine, the littlest ones flapping their wings anxiously at the end of the line. "Does it trouble you that we haven't any children, André?"

He was silent for a moment, trying to work out the words. Sophie was sometimes sad that she had been unable to have a baby. "I loved a child once," André said finally, "until I fell in love with her as a woman. It is more than enough, to have loved both in the same body."

Several weeks later the scientists at the Institute hurried to open the package that had arrived from Madame Blanchard. They gave no thought to the note or the barometer and thermometer inside; they cared only about her chart.

Unrolling it, they got right to work.

Half degree by half degree they started tracing Madame Blanchard's progress up the sky; each increment indicated that she had risen one hundred and forty feet. They decided, quite rightly, that she had made no drawings of the lower regions because she had flown within the clouds and been unable to see them.

But on a separate page they found two small sketches of cloud formations. The French word for *threadlike* was written next to one and *feathered* was beside the other.

The scientists were puzzled. They were used to Latin names and they knew Madame Blanchard was too. Then they remembered that sometimes she had mentioned Lamarck and that he had used French words. But when they looked up his five categories of clouds, though the names were equally odd, like "dappled," and "broomlike," they did not include hers.

The men turned back to the chart and continued to graph her climb into the upper regions. When they finished, they were astonished. Madame Blanchard had traveled eighteen thousand feet up the sky. Nearly four miles! And in temperatures as low as minus 8.6 degrees! At the bottom of the chart—and at the top of her flight—were written the two words she had placed next to her drawings. "Threadlike" and "feathered" were what she called the two new cloud forms she had seen at that great altitude.

Only later, when they found Madame Blanchard's note, did the scientists understand that she had named them in honor of Lamarck. And that while she thanked the men of the Institute, she had no further use for their barometer and thermometer.

⌒

28

WEARING OTHER HATS

IN HIS CHÂTEAU IN ST. CLOUD, Napoleon sat at his writing table with his head in his hands.

Since February he had lost Warsaw, Berlin, Hamburg, and Dresden.

Now it was April, and he still hadn't even gone to the front!

What was he waiting for? Napoleon asked himself.

In Russia the year before, after a long, cold march east, he had ridden up a hill on the Moscow road and seen the city spread out beneath him. The thousands of domes and cupolas decorated in gold and fairy-tale colors and the row upon row of wooden houses had looked like toys. They had been his to play with, like Isabey's coronation dolls—until he had allowed the Russians to evacuate the city.

The next day they had set fire to Moscow!

The wooden houses had burned like kindling and the domes and cupolas had flamed like candles. In fields outside the city Napoleon had seen Russians fueling fires with gilt frames as if they were scrap.

The scene had devastated him, far more than the sight of the piles of dead bodies, or carts filled with amputated limbs, or doctors reduced to dressing wounds with paper and birch-bark fiber, or horses ridden to death.

It had made him afraid to fight! Napoleon realized suddenly.

Rapping his hand on the table, he stood.

Russia was a debacle he would put behind him with the next drum roll.

He shouted to Constant to start packing.

Marc-Emmanuel and Isabelle had invited Daguerre and Louise for a visit, and that afternoon they were at tea on the lawn when Marc-Emmanuel pulled out a letter.

"Listen, Sophie's gardening!"

"Flowers?"

"Potatoes!"

As Isabelle passed cakes they surveyed the scene before them. In front of the tea table short, docile *fleurs de lis* fell within a lover's knot of clipped boxwood. Beyond it, topiary hares and geese pruned from dark green yews maintained the decorum of close-cut fur and smooth feathers. The sprays of pale yellow rosebuds looked as if they were climbing with abandon over the crosspieces of the pergola, but everybody knew they were as trussed as birds on a spit. On a nearby hillside workers in the vineyard picked only the leaves that shaded the young grapes.

Nothing resembled a potato patch.

"Sophie hates potatoes, doesn't she?" Marc-Emmanuel said to Isabelle. "She says they're thick. Remember how she drove us crazy in Vienna? It's all they eat."

"Does she say anything about flying?" asked Louise.

"No. I doubt she will fly again," said Marc-Emmanuel. "She writes that she enjoyed measuring out straight rows with string and planting potato eyes!"

"Rousseau was a philosopher, but he gave it up," said Isabelle. "He copied out music for the last ten years of his life. Though he drew the line at copying anything for a harpsichord. He said the music bristled with notes as painful on the eye as on the ear!"

Daguerre laughed. "Potato vines can be painful on the eye too!"

Marc-Emmanuel put away the letter. "She ends with the dove in the kitchen and the pig in the garden." He didn't know why he found it troubling, the notion of an earthbound Sophie digging in the dirt. She was like the daughter he had never had, and he was happier with her safe on the ground. But still.

In Boulogne the next morning, Sophie worked in the garden with her hoe, even though a neighbor had told her a shovel would make it easier. When André came down the towpath, he gazed at her wavering rows, her dusty bonnet, and blistered hands. He hooked a dirty curl behind her ear and laughed.

"André." This was said in a grave way. "Dance me across the village square, please." And lifting her up, he turned her around and around the garden until his boots were tangled in young potato vines.

But that afternoon, even the small green shadows of spring leafing out made Sophie feel sickish. At such times she thought of her days in the sky. Stopping to scratch a bug bite on her arm, she saw Napoleon across the river.

Why did he bother with the peasant disguise, when he was so unmistakably himself? she wondered. The Seine was too wide for them to hear each other, and he was mimicking her progress with her hoe, flinging make-believe dirt this way and that. Sophie's eyes were black slits. Why shouldn't she have a kitchen garden like everyone else?

Napoleon enjoyed his little pantomime, but when he leaned on his pretend hoe he grew thoughtful. He could understand why Sophie would refuse to fly for an emperor, but there was every reason for her to want to fly for the people of France.

The next day, on the way to Germany to begin his march on Dresden, a picture recurred.

Her straight, brave back, bending over weeds!

Three months later, at the Congress of Prague, Napoleon couldn't believe his ears. Austria was threatening to wage war on him! Hadn't he married the king's daughter just to make sure that wouldn't happen? And now the Austrian minister had the gall to tell him he shouldn't fight because he would lose too many soldiers?

"A man like me cares little for the lives of a million men!" Napoleon shouted.

He threw down his hat and waited for the Austrian minister to pick it up.

But Metternich didn't move, nor did the black bicorne.

"I will not give up one inch of ground!" Napoleon roared.

But as time went by he did, because he had to. In the days following the Congress, all of Europe arrayed itself against him. The Dutch, Belgians, Germans, and Prussians alike fell into step behind his father-in-law. When the Prussian army invaded Paris, Napoleon knew his fate was sealed.

"What will the people *say* if you abdicate?" someone asked.

"*Ouf*," said the emperor, gouging out an arm of his chair with his knife. "They will say *ouf*." He couldn't blame them. Why should people care if he was driven from his palace, when they had been driven from their homes?

Napoleon began making his way south to exile. As soon as people attacked his carriage, he put on the helmet of a guardsman and rode in front of it. The minute he was spotted, he threw on a Russian cloak and galloped off. By the time he reached the Mediterranean he had also been an Austrian cavalryman and the British commissioner Colonel Campbell.

He couldn't wait to get back into his favorite green coat and put on his black bicorne. But when he got dressed to board the ship to the island of Elba, his valet wasn't there to help him.

"Too many hats," said Louis Constant. Obscurely, some thought.

ILLUMINATIONS

BELOW, BOYS WERE leading cows and goats, and soldiers were carrying litters of wounded men. Sophie and André were on their way to Beaune, by balloon because the roads were so crowded. She hadn't piloted an airship for some time, and had forgotten the stir it caused. When people looked up, shouting and waving, some of them called her name. Waving back, Sophie remembered how she had felt the first time she had seen a balloon, in Lyon; how the people around her had smiled and so had she. It was the same feeling she had when she left the earth—a sense of lightness and freedom.

Sophie reached in her pockets.

"I think we should get higher first." André smiled as he handed her a sandbag.

When she untied it, sous spilled out. Looking at him, Sophie reached for another bag and found that he had filled all of them with coins.

As they showered money over the side, the airship grew lighter. But it didn't matter how high they flew. As clearly as if they were a few feet in the air instead of thousands, Sophie and André heard the children's laughter at the sight of the coins falling from the sky. It reminded her of other moments, of the ice storm in Boulogne when the sky had seemed to open, flooding the days with light, and strangers had smiled at strangers. And once in Milan, she had seen a light display set off from a balloon, and people had laughed and talked in the streets as they looked up at the illuminations that filled the sky.

Sophie and André had emptied all their bags of coins, and they were flying so high that it was cold; she wished they could fly still higher, though she knew it wouldn't make any difference. Along with the children's laughter and the people's shouts at the sight of their balloon, the cries of the wounded and the sounds of wagons rolling families from their homes would be as near.

Then André's arms were around her.

He spoke quietly because what he said wasn't meant for her, but Sophie heard the words echo in his chest that France was dying.

Late that afternoon, Sophie and André chanced upon an east-flowing current. As they flew low over the Duroc château, André recognized the old woman waving from the terrace. "No cane!" he said, pleased.

"How do you know her?"

"I healed her once near here, in Dijon."

They landed a mile or two away from the château, and

within half an hour Marc-Emmanuel had collected them in a carriage. When Isabelle greeted them on the lawn, Sophie walked into her mother's arms as through a garden gate. On the terrace, over a supper of cold sliced duck, the news was of Napoleon's return from exile. "People say he's crazy. Stark, staring mad. Now he's conscripting young boys and old soldiers," said Marc-Emmanuel. "I won't go, even if he orders it. The carnage! Under his command a million Frenchmen have been killed and millions more wounded. To say nothing of millions of enemy soldiers.

"France is exhausted. She can barely stand." Marc-Emmanuel stopped and shook his head. "But this is no conversation for a quiet summer night!"

For a while the talk was of the lack of rain, but then, watching fireflies glimmer on the lawn, Sophie described the illuminations she had seen in Italy. "They were fixed on frames hanging from wires thirty feet below the basket. The yellow lights looked like flecks of brilliance from beyond the sky, like glimpses of the future. Think what such a sight might mean to people here.

Later she and her mother walked in the close shade of the château's green allées.

"Do you ever think of La Salière, Maman?" Sophie asked.

"Only of a hollowed-out stone and my daughter on my lap."

Isabelle was remembering the day she had decided to leave her family's château outside of La Rochelle. She had grown up with a father who did not hesitate to whip a peasant and a mother filled with generations of disdain. Even as a young girl, Isabelle had wanted to cast her lot elsewhere; she had been sure that any life, however simple, would be better. But it was not until she was expecting a child that she had left La Rochelle.

Her daughter had set her free.

"Do you think of the air, perhaps, Maman?"

"You are my air, Sophie."

Marc-Emmanuel and André sat talking on the terrace.

"Sophie's illuminations sound dangerous," said Marc-Emmanuel.

Nodding his thanks to Berthe smiling and pouring his coffee, André thought of the people he had healed over the years. Although he had laid his hands on relatively few, he knew that many more had been helped, for curing one gave others hope. He had seen it fill their eyes. More than anyone, André understood Sophie's need to be of use. He knew what it meant to help, and what it felt like to be unable to. Recently he needed quiet before he healed and sometimes a cure required a second visit. His touch wasn't so sure, and the lines of people weren't so long, as if they knew.

How could he tell Sophie not to try to help, when she could?

André stirred cream into his coffee, and studied the design on the tablecloth. When he looked up, Marc-Emmanuel's light eyes were on his.

"Sophie was captive for years to a man she didn't love," André said at last. "I don't think she should be made captive to the wishes of the man she does, do you?"

. . .

One hot afternoon late that June, Sophie sat writing letters down by the Seine. It had taken time to work out the details for her first lighting display. She and Cusset had designed a balloon made of the strongest silk, the one with the doubled thread. Instead of varnish they had coated it with India rubber, a mixture of turpentine and rubber that would give better protection. She had corresponded with the Italian aeronaut whose display she had seen, and he had arranged for her rigging to be made. Now she wrote him that she planned four ascensions—the first in Paris, the second in Nîmes, the third in Grasse, and the last, again in Paris. Then she thanked him for his help and put down her pen. For the first time, she was glad to be well known. It meant she would draw larger crowds.

As she gathered up her things, Sophie saw Napoleon on the other bank of the Seine. He was flourishing his imaginary hoe again!

Sophie swept her hand across the empty garden, and shook her head.

No, there was no denying the sweetness of his smile as Napoleon pranced around his upraised arm that jabbed the sky in a question.

Sophie curved her arms into a balloon above her head and pirouetted in reply.

Napoleon stopped prancing and stared at her fixedly, all humor gone. Tucking his left hand in an imaginary vest, he tipped a phantom bicorne and bowed, a real bow—though high and stiff from disuse—then shoved the hat back on his head.

Never had he bowed so low or honored a woman more!

he thought. But Sophie deserved more than that; she deserved
a drum roll. Perhaps his favorite, the *pas de charge* that sounded
on the battlefield as long as men should fight. For there was
no question France needed her now.

Giving Sophie a last salute, Napolean clicked his heels and
turned to his final exile. He would not be the one to call for
the *pas de charge*. After Waterloo France had ordered his drums
stilled forever.

He didn't notice that Sophie had failed to curtsy.

Two weeks later, all over Paris, clusters of people grew.

It was the night of Sophie's first pyrotechnical display.

On the Champ-de-Mars, she had set out her equipment
and checked off the tasks as they were completed: In her
ballooning, if not in her housework, Sophie was meticu-
lous. First the wires were tested to ensure they were attached properly to the airship, next the frames were secured
to the wires, and then the lights were fastened on. The
usual safety measures for the airship were also followed,
the many knots tightened, the anchor and other necessary
tools strapped to the outside of the basket or stowed on
board. Although the preparations were accomplished with
painstaking care, the sheer quantity of wires, lines, casks of
iron filings, and barrels of sulfur conspired to a mechanical
nightmare.

But in the air an hour later, in a kind of alchemy, it was
transformed into magic.

Servant girls slipped outside for a look and were joined by
well-dressed couples stepping down from carriages. Customers

walked out of cafés forgetting to pay, and a man hoisted a little girl to his shoulder so she could see.

The next day they spoke of it almost shyly, walking into shops and crossing the street with strangers.

"Did you see?"

No one ever forgot the splashes of light that brightened the sky. The story of that night would be told over and over. It would become so embellished that in the years to come people said gold coins had cascaded down the sky and a white dove had spread its wings over all of Paris. And in a way they were right, for Sophie had filled the sky with miracles, and made some things seem possible that for so long had not.

Like the coins she took from her pockets, they were her gift to the people of France.

In Beaune one summer morning months later, Isabelle asked from her chaise longue, as she did whenever a letter arrived from Boulogne, "When does she fly next?"

"She doesn't say. But these are lovely nights for ballooning—" Marc-Emmanuel stopped, for Isabelle had moved restlessly in her chair.

Over the course of a year Sophie had produced her illuminations in Grasse and Nîmes. Each time the preparations had been the same, for she used the simplest techniques possible. Tonight, in Paris, would be the last of her four displays.

In Boulogne, fitted to André's side as usual and walking along the Seine, Sophie watched a boy in a punt put away his pole and let the current take him. It reminded her of when she and Jean-Pierre had come to Paris by barge and a houseboat with its red geraniums had floated into the past forever. Since then, she had discovered a more ample present. Though the boy was nearly in her past, she knew he would continue punting through his day. Sophie found it comforting that the present wasn't tied to her own view but to some larger pattern.

André was pushing back his hair and looking at the sky. "No wind and not many clouds." He nudged her off with his hip. "You'd better get ready."

An hour later when she waved to him, he kept sweeping out the barn and shouted, "I'll follow in an hour. We'll have supper at the Grand Véfour!"

When she had first begun to fly Sophie had realized that her instincts, developed on the ground to gauge the weight and solidity of a stone or a shell, were of no use in the air. She had seen massed fortresses yield to the slightest airs, and what seemed impregnable turn to mist. Slowly, she had learned to trust to transparency.

It was not yet noon when Sophie's entourage reached Paris. Even so, it would be well after dark before she began her ascent, for rigging the ship with its new devices was time-consuming.

Finally at nine-thirty the balloon was ready. Once she would have ridden up and around the clouds above her, but now she rose straight through them.

Watching her fly up through the clouds, André remembered when Sophie had flown through fear. She had never talked about it, and he sensed it had been hers to overcome.

But he had known, and he chastised himself for not having had the same resolve.

Loving Sophie, he had let slip a gift.

Loving her, he would try to reclaim it; he would detach a bit, from her.

More than anyone, she would understand.

Also in the crowd that evening was Jean-Baptiste Lamarck. A year or so ago, when he heard that Sophie had stopped flying, he had been glad. He thought the finest adventures—and hers was one—ought to end in return, for escape took a different form. But he also understood why she had taken up flight again. Seventy-five years old, nearly blind, able to see only a blur of shapes and colors, Lamarck could imagine the people in their bandages and tattered clothes, looking up; he knew why Sophie wanted to light a space between them and despair.

A few minutes later, the crowd saw a violet ball drop from a cloud and they cheered the start of another magnificent display. But Lamarck bowed his head at the sight of the violet blur. He was a scientist and he didn't need to hear people cry out in horror a few seconds later or see them stretch out their arms as if to catch the small figure clinging to a rope.

As André ran through the streets of Montmartre and neared the place where Sophie had fallen, he heard people saying,

Against the house at 16, rue de Provence.
On the cobblestones.
Not a mark on her.
Even from the flames and her fall.
One foot is bare.

"Mort dramatique de Mme. Blanchard"
July 6, 1819

When André reached Sophie, her face was closed as if a door had shut.

But kissing her, he felt life pulsing lightly. Holding Sophie in his arms, André thought, This is easy, I've done it a hundred times. For an instant her eyes flickered open and in them was the same blaze of feeling he had seen once before, greater than love, though love was in it, then Sophie lowered her gaze forever against his touch.

. . .

Because of the distances between one corner of Paris and another—to say nothing of the length and breadth of France— word of Sophie's death reached the cities and towns at different times. When people heard the news, often they walked outside and stood talking about Madame Blanchard and the healer she had loved. Some places were remote, a rude shepherd's hut or a run-down cottage at the end of a pasture lane. But over the years, probably Sophie had flown above those too, and when word finally got to them, the peasants stood in their doorways and gazed at the sky.

Sophie had been their emblem for freedom, and that night she became their symbol of hope.

But some people were touched more personally. The old villagers in La Salière gathered in their neighbors' cottages and talked about Sophie and André when they were young. In Lyon, Cusset raged at his strongest silk that had not been strong enough.

And in Beaune.

But even there, probably it began in the same way. In the scullery of the Duroc château, someone started to hum and another picked up the tune. It happened around a candlelit table in La Salière, in cafés and on village squares and crowded streets. For though not everyone could say it in words, they could put into song their feeling that Sophie belonged to them. Sometimes it was "Ça Ira" or an old folk song or a lullaby.

But more often that night, people all over France sang "La Marseillaise." And because of the different times they did, it became a round that continued until dawn. The night of singing helped André understand that he and the woman in his arms had belonged not only to each other, and that one day when he placed his hand on an ailing child, the child would heal.

EPILOGUE

WORD CAME FROM WEIMAR that Goethe was ill.

The day before leaving to visit him, Marc-Emmanuel decided to look after Sophie's grave. Until now, André had taken care of it, but he had died a few months before. Of pneumonia, the doctor said, though everyone was sure that wasn't so. André had given himself to the people who had come to his garden gate. Near the end, he had complained of numbness on his right side, where Sophie had always been, and was gone soon after.

In the cemetery, thick grasses were growing through the roses and vines that climbed over Sophie's mausoleum. Pulling away some ivy, Marc-Emmanuel saw a few words freshly chiseled into one side of her tomb. He must remember to tell Goethe, who always wanted the news of his circle of friends in France.

But in Weimar the talk was of potatoes.

Goethe was failing rapidly, finding it hard to speak, and

so he patted the pile of letters at his side. One after another, Marc-Emmanuel picked them up until Goethe stopped him at the one written by a Dr. Antommarchi.

On St. Helena, Antommarchi wrote, Bonaparte had been inconsolable when he had learned of Madame Blanchard's death. One day the doctor had come upon him napping in his tub and was reminded of what a visitor had said, that he looked like a fat Chinese pig. "In my hand was a gift for Bonaparte from an English admirer—seedlings of everlasting to remind him of his native Corsica. It was springtime in the southern hemisphere. I suggested he take up gardening."

Within days the former emperor's household had been a beehive of activity. In the morning first thing, Bonaparte got up the housemen, the cook, the coachman, and the stable boys and turned them all outside. Hopes ran high among the amateurs as they scurried about planting a botanical paradise, and Bonaparte had goaded them into working even harder. He had trained his water pipe on laggards, chortled, sworn, and threatened.

But St. Helena had an unhealthy quality even on the best of days. Longwood's pale gray terrace was often black with the stretched-out bodies of sleeping rats. There were no birds to speak of, so insects led long lives, and that year they ate steadily through the former emperor's flowers and vegetables. Then too, the air on the island was moist and humid, and decomposition was rapid among the fleshy plants like amaryllis and plumbago. But despite humidity, it seldom rained, so the sweet alyssum got hot feet and the ginger lost its spice.

One day when Bonaparte went out to look at his potato plants (Antommarchi followed this with several question marks) he saw the vines had turned yellow—a melancholy sign of what lay beneath.

The former emperor went back inside and ate his luncheon in the tub.

The servants stopped raking and got back to polishing the silver.

Gardening at Longwood had come to an end and Dr. Antommarchi came to the point.

He was considering writing a book about Bonaparte's last days on St. Helena (who wasn't! he joked) and was certain his garden had been meant to honor Madame Blanchard. Knowing of the poet's friendship with Bonaparte and the lady aeronaute, Antommarchi wondered if Goethe could shed light on the question: *Why potatoes?*

Goethe's eyes echoed Antommarchi's confusion.

"I'll tell you why," said Marc-Emmanuel.

There are crowds down there! he had told André, opening the garden gate one day a year or so after Sophie's death. He had seen soldiers with dirty bandages, women holding silent babies, and old men leaning against trees. There seemed no end to the work André had to do.

A brother came at half after six to take them to the priory for supper and a good night's sleep, André said; they would return in the morning and wait their turn down by the Seine.

As the two old friends sat on the terrace that evening, Marc-Emmanuel was peering into the dusk when a handsome old pig with a scar on his forehead walked up the terrace steps and stood in front of André.

Behind him in the garden, vines sprawled everywhere.

"Potato vines!" Marc-Emmanuel said. "Sophie planted a patch one summer, and I guess André and Bonaparte both found it touching, her digging in the dirt."

"André's housekeeper says he hated potatoes, but planted them every year, regular as clockwork," said Daguerre, walking into the room. "But I've come to show you another memorial." He looked at Marc-Emmanuel. "The last time I was here in Weimar, Goethe tapped his notes for *Faust*. He kept tapping until I picked them up, and then he stopped me at a certain line."

Opening a leather case, Daguerre drew out a metal plate.

It was one of his first daguerreotypes.

"'An angel redeems those who constantly strive,'" Marc-Emmanuel read. "I just saw that on Sophie's mausoleum!"

"I had it carved a few months ago. That was what you wanted, wasn't it?" Daguerre asked Goethe.

The poet nodded. The idea was important to *Faust*; it had come to him years ago, in a dream about Sophie. Then Goethe studied the silvered metal. He had never seen such a thing, though he and Daguerre had discussed the possibility many times.

Later, when he was alone among his portraits of old friends, Goethe's eyes rested on a drawing Daguerre had made of Sophie, her features alight against her black curls. One of Goethe's pleasures was collecting pictures, and hundreds of them—etchings, watercolors, paintings, and caricatures—shone in the candlelight. Some were no more than a hasty sketch or a single expressive line but in each one, even in a simple landscape, he had seen something of the artist.

But where on the metal plate was the artist Daguerre? he wondered.

Goethe was an old theater man, and to him the daguerreotype looked like the wrong prop on a stage set, from the wrong period and therefore troubling to the eye. It might even be ahead of its time, he thought, for his warm cluttered room suddenly seemed old-fashioned and out of date.

That night, sitting in his favorite armchair, Goethe seemed to drift through a waking dream. From the few words he managed, a visiting friend thought he saw an image—a drawing or a painting perhaps. He mentioned a woman with black hair, in curls, and a face in shadows against a black background.

"More light!" cried Goethe just before he died.

No one knew what he meant.

Goethe had been a man of many parts, and for all anybody knew, he could have been ordering more light on his stage. But of course he was a poet as well and he had lived through dark years; he might have been voicing a need for wisdom greater than the world possessed. Yet he was also an old man, with the end only a breath away, and possibly he felt that darkness was encroaching too quickly.

His words would remain a mystery.

But as the women who gossiped at the well in La Salière liked to say, *one thing was certain*.

That day Goethe's memories had been of Sophie, and perhaps, with the talk of her little mausoleum and her potatoes, he had been reminded of the light she had glimpsed beyond a fissured sky.

HISTORICAL NOTE

Taken together, the archives in France at Le Bourget's Musee de l'Air, in Les Petits-Andelys, La Rochelle, and Rochefort, as well as in America in the Manuscript Division of the Library of Congress and in the Smithsonian Museum's Department of Lighter Than Air, present a fairly complete history of Sophie Armant Blanchard's life and that of her husband, Jean-Pierre.

I gleaned from these accounts that he was cranky, slightly paranoid, and frightened in the air at times, while she was beloved for her generosity and her daring. In writing *The Little Balloonist*, I drew on the details of their flights found in the newspapers of the day. But beyond that, Sophie and Jean-Pierre are figments of my imagination.

Napoleon is something of a different story. I did my best to have his actual character and idiosyncrasies very much on the page. He did prefer white on a woman, was horrified by an open door, and was inclined to spend long hours in the bath. The reader may trust to my account of him—his letters to Joséphine, his feelings about Moscow, his disguises—in almost every respect save that of his love for Sophie. But, since he did admire courage above all things, and since she actually was his daring and official balloonist, who is to say he *didn't* harbor a love her, however secret?

I tried to fit Napoleon's passion for Sophie into the pattern of his life, disrupting it as little as possible.

In addition to his love for Sophie, there is another instance in which I took liberties with Napoleon's biography. Talma was indeed an actor and his friend but other than an amusing scene I once saw in a movie about Napoleon, I have no reason to believe Talma gave him acting lessons on courtship.

The account of André Giroux's healing in the Vendée was based on the news report of a healer in La Rochelle in the 1860s. I used it nearly verbatim for my "article" in *Le Moniteur de Saintonge* because I was impressed—and startled—by the sincerity of the correspondent.

The characters of Daguerre, Goethe, and Lamarck are not contrived. That is to say, I tried to remain true to what is known about them. As with Napoleon, excepting their relationship with Sophie, what I wrote about them is based on fact; perhaps most significantly Goethe's last day and his last words. However, as far as I know, Goethe's mother was not enamored of Jean-Pierre Blanchard, nor was Rousseau Sophie's father.

The events in the story—the battles, uprisings, conditions of life in France, and so on—accord with historical fact. Several books were the mainstays of my research. They are distinguished by being colorful as well as factual: Jean-Paul

Kauffmann's *The Black Room at Longwood*; Simon Schama's *Citizens*; Alan Schom's *Napoleon Bonaparte*; Frank McLynn's *Napoleon*; Ernest Knapton's *Empress Josephine*; Diana Reid Haig's *Walks Through Napoleon and Josephine's Paris*; Charles Gillispie's *The Montgolfier Brothers and the Invention of Aviation*. There is a snippet of borrowed history I am unable to attribute. The little barge children were real, but for the life of me I can't remember where I read about them; my apologies to their chronicler.

For all its historical trappings and famous inhabitants, the story of Sophie Blanchard is a fable.

It was delicious to make, and I hope it pleases.

ILLUSTRATIONS

Grateful acknowledgment is made to the following for permission to reprint etchings:

Vaisseau Volant Aerostatique de Mr. Blanchard, page 21, courtesy of the Smithsonian Institution. SI Neg. No.85-18304: National Air and space Museum, Smithsonian Institution (SI 85-18304).

Montgolfier in courtyard with balloon, page 37, courtesy of the Smithsonian Institution. SI Neg. No.2003-35049: National Air and Space Museum, Smithsonian Institution (SI 2003-35049).

Premier Passager Arien de Jean-Pierre Blanchard, page 59, courtesy Library of Congress, Prints and Photographs Division, LC-USZ62-104588.

Engraving depicting destruction of balloon, page 73, courtesy of the Smithsonian Institution. SI Neg. No.2002-20291:

National Air and Space Museum, Smithsonian Institution (SI 2002-20291).

Napoleon Bonaparte, circa 1809, page 106, courtesy Butler Library, Columbia University in the City of New York.

Ascension de Madame Blanchard au Champ-de-Mars 1810, page 167, courtesy of the Smithsonian Institution. SI Neg. No.74-7554: National Air and Space Museum, Smithsonian Institution (SI 74-7554).

Mort Dramatique de Mme. Blanchard, July 6, 1819, page 189, courtesy of the Smithsonian Institution. SI Neg. No.92-14974: National Air and Space Museum, Smithsonian Institution (SI 92-14974).

ACKNOWLEDGMENTS

A number of friends read drafts of *The Little Balloonist*. Early on, I appreciated the encouragement of Polly and John Guth; later, from their different creative perspectives, Steve Kellogg, Nancy Nicholas, and Franny Taliaferro suggested ways to strengthen the narrative. Other friends, among them Elsie Aidinoff, Barbara Ascher, Jill Broderick, Katherine Cary, Constance Fulenwider, Pam Howard, Elizabeth Hunnewell, K.C. Hyland, Dr. Montie Mills, and Annie Rohrmeier, were kind enough to read the manuscript and inquire after its progress as one might a child: "How's Sophie?" In addition, I want to thank two friends especially. Lucy Borge and Gordy Woodhouse patiently familiarized themselves with several drafts, for which I am grateful. My thanks also to my longtime friend Judy Wilson, who helped me at moments to parse the logic of this story; to Elise Frick, whose questions I had then to answer; to my brother Paul Lewis, for weighing in with some difficult math; to Chantal Berman, for singing a little

French lullaby; and to my friend Dr. William Fowler, who shared my awe at those early, intrepid aviators.

Through Gordy, I met my agent, Catherine Drayton of Inkwell Management, whose professional interest in *The Little Balloonist* naturally meant a great deal. Also at Inkwell, my thanks to Kim Witherspoon, whose comments on the manuscript were most helpful. Rosemary Ahern provided commentary on an early draft, and I thank her for her enthusiastic response to Sophie's story. I appreciate the help of Janet Foster and Joshua McKeon in trying to keep me from straying too far from actual fact.

In the Smithsonian Museum's Department of Lighter Than Air, my thanks to Allan Janus for his unfailing courtesy and for his help in obtaining visuals, and to Tom Crouch for his voluminous knowledge, equaled only by his sheer love of flight.

To my editor, Julie Doughty, my thanks for being clear-thinking, patient, and a pleasure to work with at every juncture.

And to my husband, Tony, and my children, Cassin and Alex, more than thanks for treating Sophie as a member of the family during the years she lived with us, though perhaps only I will be sad to see her leave.

ABOUT THE AUTHOR

Linda Donn is author of two critically acclaimed works of nonfiction, *The Roosevelt Cousins: Growing up Together, 1882–1924* (Knopf, 2001) and *Freud and Jung: Years of Friendship, Years of Loss* (Scribner, 1988), which was translated into seven languages. This is her first novel. She lives in New York.